MANE GUARDA

The Twins of Sanescid

The Oracle Children

First edition

Editing by Melanie Scott

This book was professionally typeset on Reedsy.
Find out more at reedsy.com

Contents

Prologue

**Have you ever imagined waking up one day in a com-
pletely different world and time** that you don't even recognize? Then you wake up again in your everyday world and
you are the same person you've always been, but now, you are
not sure which one is the real you?

It all starts when I begin having very strange dreams. I'm
not much of a writer, but if I didn't record this period of my
life I thought I would go crazy. It is September 3rd, 2003. I'm
not sure if the dreams are set long ago or in a parallel world.
There are different types of humans that do not seem to mix
with each other, and if they do, their babies are cursed, seen
as aberrations, and not acknowledged by society. Worse, they
mean trouble. For instance, if there is a flood, an earthquake, or
any disaster, it is blamed on these poor creatures, and therefore,
they are punished. At the same time, though, they would never
dare kill them. They fear to be cursed by the Oksaleb for the
rest of their lives. Who are the Oksaleb? Everybody believes
that they are delegates of the Gods. So, these poor hybrids
survive as they can, usually hiding in the streets of a city or in
the wild. Many are taken as slaves. Luckily, there are very few
of them.

The dreams are so real that I wake up remembering everything, even the details. I dream I'm a queen (they call me "My
Anier") of a place named Sanescid. In the first dream, I'm

pregnant with my second child. My first is a beautiful five-year-old daughter, Ariadne. We are going to the Naming Ceremony, which all pregnant women have to attend. It's a very simple ritual where we have to drink a concoction in the presence of a few chosen members of our family or friends. The ceremony is held in a temple. I choose Nekane, my companion and best friend, because my family lives too far away. I let my husband Kuiril choose the other person. He chooses Daedalus, his best friend, King of Heinne. Daedalus is a very charming man, but for some reason I don't trust him. He seems false and the kind of person that never grows up: very selfish, as if everything was created for him.

The concoction is hallucinatory, but it usually doesn't harm the mother, nor the child. If it does, we believe that it was meant to be. We sit in a circle and make a little prayer: "Oh, Oracle, tell us the truth. Please let it be good news, oh God of gods!" I drink; it has a bitter taste. It takes some time to take effect, so we make small talk.

"Are you scared?" says Daedalus, with a smirk on his face.

"No," I say. "This is my second time." I had done it when pregnant with Ariadne and had had a good experience. The Oracle then had stated that Ariadne was going to be a queen, and a very good one at that.

"Have you dreamed of our baby?" says Kuiril.

I haven't. I'm five months pregnant, so it is strange that it hasn't happened yet. "No. Let's hope that it's not a bad omen," I say.

I start feeling dizzy and start hearing a voice in my head, "Close your eyes and focus on your *arima*," it says. I know this is the word for 'soul.' "Nothing is under your control." Then I have a vision of red rain falling on two babies. They have friendship was not real. I will not stand for it anymore. I'll ask her to leave. She'll probably try to take my place, luring my husband. That will be funny. Kuiril is not the kind to fall in love. That's never going to happen. The king of Sanescid is very caste-oriented. I was the noblest of the nobles. He will never go for something less. I bet that he'll stick with me no matter what, even if we never see each other again. I can't even imagine him telling my family about this. It seems that we will have to make a deal, but the love between us will never come back. I feel the unfairness of it like a pain in my heart. Why did that freak baby have to be born? Why am I accused of something I never did? How can I prove my innocence? Oh gods! I can only calm my pain with wine.

Then I'm back to the present. I don't even know the babies' names.

My doctor, as I anticipated, does not take my worry seriously. After my last dream, I'd woken up with a bad headache, so I try to convince him that there must be something wrong.

"What if I have a tumor?" I say.

"If so, I would be able to see it just through the regular examination we've already done." He adds, "I think this has more to do with stress or perhaps your menopause, Mrs. Blight."

"Please," I say. "This one time!"

Canada has a medical insurance system where the family doctor is the one that decides whether you need a specialist or any special exam. Otherwise you have to pay, which can be very expensive. I'm trying to convince him to let me get a CAT scan. Luckily, he consents, since I hadn't had any exams for years.

Ulrich, my real husband, recommends that I write about

the dreams. "You could track down the connection between them and your migraines. On the other hand, if they are as interesting as what you've been telling me, you could write them as a story. Worst case scenario, it'll be for your personal benefit," he says.

It's great advice. Why not?

A month has passed and I dream again. The CAT scan results are negative, which is good news. I prefer to have a loose screw, but be perfectly healthy, than be crazy and sick. The next time I dream I learn the names of the babies, who are toddlers by then. They have named the first one, the Oksaleb, Zigor, which means punishment, and the second is Sendoa, meaning strong. I learn this from the servants, for I have no access to them (I might have been allowed to see Zigor, but I don't care to). Actually, I don't care to see anybody. I'm in a permanent state of semiconsciousness because of my drinking. I see two, no, three empty jugs rolling on the floor. I look under the bed, my head feeling like it is going to split in two. Either I'm seeing things or there are two more jugs under the bed. Damn, I want to die! I hear what sounds like a pounding noise at the door, though it's probably a mere rap.

"Who's that?" I say, in a rasping voice, I don't think anybody can hear me. My headache is so intense that I can barely speak. I know that the solution is more wine, but I've emptied every single jug. This must be hell. "Please, come in," I say with an effort, hoping that whoever it is will be the last living creature I see. Then I throw up, though nothing comes out, just one gag after another.

It's Erlea, the maid who's been given the job of taking care of me. She enters. "My Anier, please stop drinking, you're killing yourself! Please, do it for your Ariadne!" she says beseechingly.

"What for, Erlea? I don't ever see my Ariadne. I don't ever see anybody I ever loved. What's the use, tell me!" I say.

"Aniero Kuiril will forgive you, I know he will, as I am here!" she says and starts to clean my face with care. She cleans my tears, and the vomit stuck around my chin. She sends for another servant to pick up the jugs on the floor and to clean. My headache is so bad, and I start gagging again.

"No, no, no, My Anier!" She gives me a cup of water, makes me drink it little by little, one sip at a time, and it works, at least for a while.

She takes me to the baths and cleans me. As she's rubbing my skin, I leave my body and float. It's a medium-sized room with a pool in the center. It's not as beautiful as the one I used to bath in with my husband before. It's simpler. The murals are mosaics portraying common people doing domestic jobs, like cleaning, taking care of children, and cooking. An apprentice beside the cook, a young girl watching the work, other girls and young lads carrying buckets of water or milk. All these activities are decorated with trees and hills in a very naïve style, but very beautiful in their way. The floor is of polished stone. There are a few chairs and a table where all the clothes are placed. On one chair is something like a sheet that will be used to dry my body. I drift away from that room to the other spaces in the castle. I can see the kitchen, people rushing to and fro, anxious to be ready on time. I wonder why they are in such a hurry. Is there a special event? Somebody visiting? I hear a thud, then a loud cry, and somebody yelling and beating somebody. I drift in that direction and see what all the fuss is. It's a child. He must have been in the way. He has been pushed to the floor and the poor thing is crying in pain. Without any consideration for the child a man is yelling, "Why are you always in the way, you stupid bastard!" He keeps on beating him. It's shocking and I wish I could do something.

"Stop, you brute!" I shout angrily, but he can't hear me. It's as if I weren't there, as if I were a ghost. I float back to myself, frustrated, desperately trying to express my anger and pain.

Back inside my body I feel bothered by that annoying cry. "Oh, for the gods' sake, who's making that child cry? My head's going to burst! Make him shut up!" I implore.

"Yes, My Anier," says Erlea, and she rushes out. I'm floating again and see how hard she is on the man who's hurting the child, "Stupid ass! Do you want to kill him? You'll see what'll happen to you and all your descendants!"

"What will happen, Erlea?" he says, fixing an icy look on her.

"If you kill that child you're angering the Oksaleb gods…" she says. Everybody knows the threat.

He spits at the child, who is now hugging his own knees, rocking himself back and forth as he tries not to cry. It's Zigor! I have no idea why, but I recognize him, even though he's probably three years old now, such a skinny little child, naked and dirty. He's full of scabs and bruises. You can see a stain where the tears are falling from his eyes to his cheeks and chin. It is the infamous mark of the Oksaleb, and I feel the shock of his birth all over again. "Maybe you should send him to his sister Ariadne. She might hide him from more punishment," I say in Erlea's ear, hoping that she can listen to me, a ghost.

"Go to your sister," she tells Zigor. "Stop bothering in the kitchen."

I'm back in my body. I don't always have control of myself. I realize that some time has passed. So, here I am, a wretched woman trying to enjoy the moment with Erlea. She's looking for a nice dress I might like to wear and I let her do it. I let her pamper me like no one has done in a lifetime. She really thinks I'm dying! I hope she is right, but I know it's not happening because I'll never get away from this hell.

"I'll talk to My Aniero. I can't believe the gossip I hear!" she says. "I know you have never looked at any other but your husband. This is ludicrous!"

"No, sweet Erlea! He will dismiss you! What would I do without you? Give me at least the comfort of having you with me! You are my eyes and ears..." I don't care what the world thinks about me anymore. I'm a drunk, for the gods' sake!

"What use is that? The news I bring you is always so bad and you end up drinking like a vulgar person, My Anier. I love you and I'm sick of seeing how you're wasting yourself away! If not by talking to My Aniero, how can I help you?" she asks.

"He will fire you and you won't find a job ever again. Trust me, I know him well enough. He will feel insulted by your comments and you'll regret it the rest of your life. Don't you see that it's him who's spreading the rumors? Who else wants me in hell with a good excuse? Also, remember what happened to Nekane. She thought she could take my place, poor devil. I told her..."

"But she deserved it," Erlea says. "How could she compare herself to you? She was too ambitious."

"Please, please don't do it!" I say. "I know my husband. He has no patience for this. Don't hurt yourself, my dear Erlea." So, there was more gossip about me, I thought bitterly. As if I could get out of this jail or some magical creature could come and visit me to do bad things. I don't care anymore, my friend. But I was lying to myself. Otherwise, why was I drinking so much?

I land back in my real life with a horrible headache. *No Erlea to take care of me here,* I thought wryly. *I'll have to call in sick.* I think that these dreams and my headaches have something in common after all. Do I wake with a headache every time I've had any of these specific dreams? Not really. I look back and realize that it's after I've had one of the dreams where I've been drinking. So, I begin to see a connection: When I have a hangover inside the dream, I wake up with the worst headaches.

Next thought: Does this happen because I've dreamt about having a hangover, or am I having a splitting headache while I'm dreaming, and therefore my brain recreates it as a hangover in the dream?

It's March 2004 and I wake again with a terrible headache. I get up to throw up, and drag myself back to bed. Passing by Ulrich's office, I ask, "What time is it, love?"

He looks at me. "Only seven. You ok?" He has been reading one of the papers he's working on, which has given him the other type of headache, the one where he knows that something is not right, but he can't put a finger on where yet.

"No. Feel like crap, again! Had another of those horrible dreams! Erlea has told me that the freak son I've told you about was taken away, given to a king in a province called Heinne. I find it so unfair! Poor kid! What on earth is going to happen to that little soul? So, in my dream, I continue to drink, even more than before if that was possible," I say. "That's why I can barely stand. I wonder if I'm going crazy! I think it's time to go to a shrink."

He laughs, "You are not going crazy. Your dreams are clearly weird, but everything you do on a regular basis is normal. I don't see you talking to the air or doing weird stuff. But if it would make you feel better…" He reaches out and caresses me.

I'm so lucky to have such a sweet guy by me.

"By the way, how's your paper coming up?" I say.

"Much better. Seems that I've finally found the problem."

I go back to bed. Luckily this time it's Sunday. I sleep for at least four more hours, and wake up much better, which is perfect because, I have to correct my students' language arts tests and plan for the week.

A week later I have probably, or I should better say, hopefully, the last dream. I think and hope so because in the dream I die. It's clear that many years have passed. Even though I can't see myself in a mirror, I can see and recognize Erlea, by then my best and only friend. She's grown thinner, her face has many more wrinkles, and her beautiful red hair is mixed with gray. I still find her beautiful and as sweet as always. She's trying to give me something to drink. I think my head is about to explode, but I try not to show it. She has tried so hard all these years to save me from myself. I know that this time I will win, but I want to show her my respect. I know I'm dying, but I try to make her feel that she's healing me. I try to drink her concoction, I really do, but my throat doesn't respond. I lose consciousness and suddenly I see myself from above. Ah, I'm floating again. Floating out of my body has come to be my only pleasure during all these years. It is as if I have wings to fly me to freedom. It would be good to check what's going on today, since it's maybe my last one, so I float out of the room straight to where my family is supposed to be. I look for Ariadne. She's the only child I have ever been given the chance to see, at least for her birthdays. She was always a very sweet girl and the only one that ever sent me her love. I can't find her inside the *gaztelu*. Since I feel so free to go anywhere, I leave the building and start roaming around, trying to find my child. I let my instinct go through me and suddenly I see her. I've floated to the market, quite a few miles away. She's all grown now. I wonder why Kuiril hasn't married her off yet. Maybe the most powerful kings are not available yet? Such an ambitious, stupid man. She'll end up wasting herself away because of him. What a wretched family we are!

She looks towards me and I wonder if she can see me. Probably not. She advances towards me and calls, but not my name. She's saying, "Zigor! Is it you?" I turn around, trying to figure out what she's looking at, and then I see. It *is* Zigor, dressed in rags, with a huge basket on his head. Beside him, a woman buying fruit. The woman tells him something. He sees me, no, Ariadne, and he moves away very fast, as if trying to disappear. My God, what did they do to that poor boy! Ariadne tries to follow, passing directly through me. She stops, looks around and then continues after Zigor. I wonder if she felt anything. I also wonder what Zigor is doing there. Those huge baskets are the type servants carry to help their masters with very heavy loads. He was given away years ago. Was he a slave, or did he work independently in the market? What is he doing in Sanescid? Isn't he supposed to be in Heinne? So many questions that will never be answered. My daughter, apparently, is trying to contact him, but he doesn't seem interested. Why should he? What did his own family ever give him, but grief? What have we given him? Nothing.

I wonder what's become of his twin, Sendoa. I float back to the palace towards the possible places he could be. I've haven't seen him since he was born, but I'm sure he must look very much like Zigor. On the way, I see one of the royal carriages entering. I wonder who's in it. It's clearly someone important because it's surrounded by soldiers. I follow. It stops by the fencing grounds. And there I can see my other son, dressed in the finest warrior's clothes. He looks very proud, but very bitter at the same time. I wonder what kind of life Kuiril gave him. *The Prince and the Pauper.* What a contrast between the brothers!

I've seen my three children. I'd like to have said goodbye. Ariadne seemed interested in taking care of Zigor, who has had no option but to do what others make him do. A prince sold as a slave, and what did I do? Nothing. Zigor was the reason for all my drinking. Blaming him, I invited hell, and hell was what he and I got, except that he was an innocent creature, born in the wrong place and time, and didn't deserve my evil wishes. My gods! I'm the worst mother in the world! Why didn't I fight for his rights as a child prince? Not even as a normal child would he deserve what he has to put up with. Oh gods, I didn't even try! What is going to happen to me now? I know I'm dying. Who's going to come to my funeral? I hope nobody. How could I neglect that child so much? Gods, gods, gods, I'm dying and haven't been able to lessen his life's burden! "Ariadne!" I hear my voice croak. I'm back in my wasted body. I never thought a body could hurt so much. I REALLY WANT TO DIE.

Erlea runs to my side. "We are looking for her!" she says, tears rolling down her cheeks.

She has no idea where Ariadne is. They won't find her on time and it doesn't matter.

My dearest daughter, I know I don't have to tell you this: Take care, as much as you can, of your pauper little brother. But how tall and handsome he looks, even with the scars! He was clearly from another world, from the Oksalebs, so hated, but so beautiful at the same time. Maybe, if I pray for him, he will have at least a better life than what I have seen so far.

I see myself out of my body again; I float towards it, trying to get in, as I had done many times, but this time I bounce back. I struggle back to myself, yet bounce back again. I float up and I see my dearest Erlea, crying and hugging my body. Up, and I see the *gaztelu* with all its splendor. Up, and I can see the city of Sanescid, its market full of people, the temples, rich houses, poor houses, the streets with children playing.

1

Munich

September 8, 2010. 5pm. Alte Pinakothek, Munich. It was getting dark and people were beginning to leave work to go to their homes. As the offices emptied, the gallery was filling up. There was an outstanding exhibition on different surrealistic artists, with a rare opportunity to see many famous works in the same place. Aileen and Ulrich were running late, which was very frustrating because they knew that it was going to be full. They were appointed to be there at 5:30—if they arrived late they would miss the exhibition altogether.

"Gawd, what was I thinking!" said Aileen. Losing her glasses just before they had to go had been stupid enough. Then, they had gotten lost and were having a hard time figuring out where they were. It was easy to ask for directions. All those phrasal dictionaries were excellent for that. The problem was understanding the directions that the very nice people were saying in German. They understood precisely nil.

So, they said, *"Danke schön,"* but couldn't follow the directions. Finally, somebody who had been observing the couple for a while told them in perfect English where they had to go. It was only three blocks away, straight and then to the right.

Getting in was another matter. There were two enormous lines and it was difficult to know what they were for, so Ulrich decided to stay in one of the lines while Aileen went to try and find out which they were supposed to be in. She managed to get to a booth, where they told her that they could get straight in. She waved Ulrich over and they entered the gallery. On the way in, they got a headphone set so that, if they chose, they could listen to the history of some of the pictures in English.

The exhibition had surrealist art from all the greats, such as Dalí, Picasso, André Breton, and Max Ernst, as well as contemporary artists such as Vivienne Wills, Stephan Korbe (all artist names are fictitious, except fort he well known ones) , and others Aileen and Ulrich hadn't heard of. What was most exciting about the event was that some of the artists exhibiting were right there, talking to the public.

The first section was, of course, dedicated to the fathers of Surrealism. It was an absolute delight to see all of their work together and have a chance to compare them. However, Aileen and Ulrich were also looking forward to seeing the new artists. They had heard so many good things about them that they wanted to see their work with their own eyes. Of course, Vivienne Wills was the first on their list, being the most feted among the new generation. Her main theme was waste: the use of waste in art. There were pieces of plastic and paper bags pasted in such a way that, when watched from far, a beautiful dreamy landscape of nature could be seen, whereas, if standing to one side, something completely different formed, something nightmarish. Ernst Voges (fictitious too) theme, on the other hand, was Germanic myths. He used mainly oils. There were others that were not so interesting.

"In any exhibition, it's only ten percent good art," commented Ulrich. Aileen, while not always agreeing on which pieces of art did have merit, agreed on the percentage, though in this exhibition she was definitely finding much more good art than a mere ten percent.

They were walking through the last gallery when she froze. The third picture to her left was an exact copy of the picture she had seen in one of her dreams. It didn't matter that seven years had passed. That image would never leave her. The picture captured two images—like feathers facing each other as if reflected in a mirror, except that one seemed blurry. Aileen looked as close to the picture as possible and noticed that the blurry image looked more like a leaf. Big drops of red, like rain, fell diagonally on both. Aileen looked at the label. *"It was never a reflection."* Artist: Zig Sanescid.

"Sanescid," she murmured. She had shivers down her back.

"What?" said Ulrich.

"Look at this picture. Remember what I told you about a picture that I dreamt about? The one I'd drawn in that dream?"

"Yeah," he said, scrutinizing the painting.

"Check the artist's name," she said, "Zig Sanescid."

"Wasn't that the name of the city you dreamed about?" said Ulrich.

"It is." She added, "Look at the first name. Zig, maybe for Zigor?"

They looked at the other pictures belonging to the artist. One showed two babies separating as they grew, and their sadness. This was another of the pictures she had dreamed about. Its title was *"We were never meant to be."* Aileen realized that the paintings were a sequence. The first had two babies

3

trying desperately to reach each other. The second showed two toddlers, further away again, this time looking at one another with distrust. The third picture showed them still further away, aged probably between five and seven years old. They were looking sideways with clear hatred. In each of the three pictures, between the children there was a red puddle, which grew as they got further apart. The final picture was a big puddle of red taking up most of the frame. There was no sign of the children in this one.

After seeing Sanescid's pictures, they tried to look at the rest of the artists' works, but Aileen couldn't concentrate. She gave up and went back, devoting all her time to those haunting images.

"I think I'd like to meet the creator of these pieces, this Zig," she said finally.

As they were exiting the exhibition, they saw a room where the artists were gathered. It was full of chairs for the gallery patrons to sit and ask questions. There were a few chairs empty, so Aileen and Ulrich went in and sat. At the front, there were a number of artists sitting behind a table. Behind them on the wall was a sign that said: *"Treffen sie die künstler"* ('Meet the artists'). A few of the artists didn't know German, so there were interpreters to help them as well as the patrons. A microphone was being passed around for visitors to ask questions. When it was Aileen and Ulrich's turn, she got the microphone.

"This is a question for Zig Sanescid," she started.

"So sorry, Zig's already gone." answered the person in charge, so Aileen had no more to ask. Frustrated, she gave the microphone to Ulrich, and he passed it to the next patron. Aileen couldn't help but worry that, after seeing these pictures, her dreams were going to return. That time had been an awful period, which she did not want to repeat. Before they left the gallery, they looked at a few more pictures by the great masters.

"Look," Ulrich said. "I want this one for my birthday." He was trying to raise her spirits.

She smiled, "I'll give it to you for Christmas, but only if you give me Zig's collection."

"You sure?" He shot her a worried look.

"No!" she said.

At the exit there was a guestbook for the visitors to make comments, and a basket where people were leaving their business cards. Aileen had no card, so she decided to leave Zig a note.

Once they left the gallery, they were exhausted so they went straight back to their hotel.

They had decided to come to Munich together. Ulrich had meetings to attend the week before. The surrealist exhibition had been a very good excuse to vacation together, after the meetings were over. Aileen had planned the week's activities. The Pinakothek had been the first one. The next day, they were planning to visit the Nymphenburg Palace. This was the main summer residence of the Bavarian rulers. It had been built at the birth of Maximilian II Emanuel, in the seventeenth century. The photos she had seen in the brochure showed a beautiful stone building and a view worthy of making the trip. The day after that, they were taking the train to Paris.

Aileen had a hard time going to sleep that night, terrorized that she could have another one of those dreams. She wondered how it was that those pictures were there at all. In the dream, she had made them. How was it that "Zig" had them? Did he make them? The same pictures, for God's sake! How could that be?

When she woke up, Ulrich had already got up. *I guess I did sleep after all. I never felt him getting out of bed*, thought Aileen. He was probably reading the newspaper he'd found in front of the door the night before. She got up, showered, grabbed her e-book and went to meet him in the Lobby. The newspaper was tossed on the floor beside him.

"How long have you been out here?" she said.

"Not long. I slept a lot!"

"Huh! But you finished the newspaper already?"

"It wasn't very interesting," he said.

"Would you like to come for breakfast with me?"

Ulrich usually didn't like to have breakfast, but this time he liked the idea of having a fruit juice.

2

Belonging

I t was the middle of the night and he was shivering on the debris, naked. Where was he? He thought he was dead and in hell. "So, hell has a specific noise?" he thought. He looked at the sky, trying to find where the noise was coming from. A noise he had never heard before. There were two floating shiny things he had never seen before either, shooting light rays at each other, and he was right under them. Suddenly, both disappeared. "So, this is hell!" But the pain in his body told him how wrong he was. He was still very much alive. He tried to get up but couldn't. There was excruciating agony in his right hip and he couldn't move that leg. "Broken," he thought. "I'll die like a street dog after all." Not too different than how he had lived anyway, which was ok. Now, he could see only one flying object almost right on top of him. He had been watching it moving very slowly. He was more curious than scared. The pain in his hip and all his miserable life helped him. There was a strong light emanating from the object towards him, and a horrible noise going in crescendo.

Beeb beebBEEP BEEP…

It was the alarm clock. Zig sat up abruptly, breathing in as if he was desperate for air. It had been another of his usual nightmares. He was exhausted. Too much partying the night before. "When will I learn to say no to these excruciating tiresome events?" He had a terrible hangover and he had to go to the museum again. "Why did I sign up for this?" he wondered aloud. "I don't even need it!"

"Hey, love." Jeannie was right beside him, lovingly pulling him out of his stupor. "Time to get up."

"Please, give me something for the hangover. I'm gonna puke otherwise."

She had an effervescent pill ready, fizzing in a glass of water. He took it and drank, hoping that it helped, at least a little. He was gagging, but he held back from actually being sick. He had to keep the pills down for them to take effect! "Please, give me a half-hour!" he said.

"Sure, love." Jeannie knew that when he had been drinking, she had to get him up earlier. He always needed thirty minutes to be rid of his headaches, but she could not understand why he drank so much when he didn't even seem to enjoy it. He sat and drank while watching everybody else having fun. Last night, a woman that didn't know he was with her tried to lure him to dance or leave the place and go somewhere nicer, but he'd said, "No thanks," in a gentle and polite, but absentminded, voice. No matter how beautiful and attractive the women were, or how persuasive, he always said no. On one occasion, a beautiful brunette used to getting what she wanted began to insult him. "You a fag, are you?" He looked at her as if not understanding that it was meant to be an insult, and answered, "Maybe." In truth, he wasn't interested in meeting anybody without a purpose, except for work or whatever the Oracle sent him to. He always looked so sad, she thought. In truth, she had never seen him laugh, not even smile.

They weren't really together. She had been hired to take care of him and make sure that he didn't get in trouble. She was also supposed to make sure he learned to live in this world on his own. She had been trying to introduce him to people that could help him succeed, a social network, but he wasn't interested. "Now he's working in this exhibition as if he was a servant!'" she thought. He was the artist, for the gods' sake! It could be frustrating.

"Why did I come to this stupid exhibition?" he wondered again, though he knew why. It had been the Oracle in his dream. The first time he had dreamt a message from the Oracle and followed its instructions, he'd gotten out of his horrendous life to something a little better. Finally, even out of slavery altogether, as now in this different world. From then on, he would always listen, respect, and follow the Oracle's instructions, no matter how weird, stupid, or insane they seemed. Now he was supposed to meet a middle-aged woman, if he wanted to begin his healing, whatever that meant—he didn't think of himself as sick. He would meet this woman only if he came to Munich, to this specific gallery at around this time. The dream had happened a year before, so he began to research the art museum in Munich. That was how he learned about the Surrealist art exhibition and had applied. With the help of Jeannie he found out what he had to prepare.

"Zig, this is very hard work. Do you really think you are up to it?" she had said, which infuriated him. When had he not worked like a slave? He only needed her help to understand what was expected of him, so as not to fail. "What does this mean? What do they expect of me? What is Surrealism?" He showered her with questions and listened attentively to every word as she explained the concept of Surrealism and what he had to have in his portfolio, step by step.

"You already have the most important piece," she had said. "All your work is surrealistic." He drew and painted images of his dreams. He had to sign in, write a profile of himself, a resume and, most important, references, which he already had because he had already shown his work locally and had been very successful. He had to show samples of all his work and describe the theme of his presentation. He had no idea what he was going to present, but he came up with something on the spot as he visualized his mother, father, sister, twin brother, or rather their absence and the pain that surrounded it all. It took he and Jeannie some time to put everything together and create what was missing, but they managed to finally send his e-portfolio a day before the deadline. He began to work on the project the next day, not worrying whether he was going to be included among the winners. He knew that he had to work very hard to finish it on time. *"It was never a reflection"* was his final title. At first, he had thought to name it *"It was never meant to be"*, but it turned into two parts and the paintings that resulted were more to do with himself and his brother, his hated twin brother.

He didn't want to think about that now. Every time he saw his own work it hurt so bad. "That must be the reason I drink so much," he thought. To forget, but he couldn't. The image of his despised brother was always watching him, accusing him, taking from him, like a bloodsucking leech. He didn't have time for that now. "Concentrate on the good things—my brother is very far away, worlds away. I'll probably never see him again," he thought, "I should be happy!" But he wasn't, and it seemed that he would never be. Actually, he didn't even

10

know what happiness was supposed to feel like. There was a hole, so big that nothing could ever fill it up. His headache was receding, so he got up and went to the shower.

When they arrived at the Pinakothek, Gervase Brenne, the assistant curator, came straight up to him. "Mr. Sanescid, we need to talk!"

Zig felt the man's anger, but he couldn't care less. "Yes?"

"You left early yesterday. Are you going to leave early today, too? Then I can leave a message to the patrons: Sorry, irresponsible artist not here, again?"

"Sorry, Mr. Brenne. It won't happen again."

"I never liked your work. The deal was that you explain it to people like me and…"

"As I said," Zig said, looking straight into the man's eyes, "this won't happen again." Then, he turned on his heel and left.

Brenne was going to go after him but decided against it. He could not like Sanescid's work, nor his attitude, but he had no power over him really. He was actually impressed at the amount of people voting for his work. Zig was one of the public's favorite among the young artists participating. 'Such a sad, pathetic work,' he thought. 'So depressing.' He could not fathom that a man so young could express so much suffering, while behaving like such an unpleasant, spoiled child.

Zig turned back to check the messages that some people had left in the guestbook. Most of them were business cards, but sometimes there were notes or even little presents. Suddenly, and for no obvious reason, he felt that he shouldn't have left early yesterday, that he had made a terrible mistake. The cards or messages were his only hope to figure out what he might have missed. He felt like he was drowning, the thought of missing what the Oracle had offered was making him sick, and the hangover did not help. He found only business cards. A few had a little message congratulating him, others asked him to save a specific piece, which he thought was stupid because he did not deal with those things and he was not planning to sell his work, yet. It was still a work in progress, at least that was how he felt at the moment. *Maybe later, when I don't care, or after I'm dead?* he thought. He knew he was good, not because of the praise people were showering on him now, but because, as a slave, he had been asked to represent the drawings of dreams or visions he had as he touched the client. He had learned to be as precise as he could, otherwise the reading could be wrong. At first, when he was caught drawing dreams on the ground with a stick, because he had felt compelled to despite knowing that it was wrong, he got a beating from his master. But when the young, rich man who had been dreaming woke up and saw the drawing on the ground, he looked desperately around for the perpetrator. He offered to pay anyone who knew who had done it. It hadn't taken long to find Zig, so he had offered his master a generous amount of coins and offered to double it if the child could tell him what it meant. Zig remembered how difficult it had been for him to move as his whole body ached from the beating. His master for the first time in his life had apologized, realizing that he had gone a bit too far. That lifted Zig's spirits, and he walked feeling a little less pain. His master knew that a slave who drew others' dreams was a capital sin, and it was not only Zig who would be put to death. But the amount of money that the stranger was offering was so much that it made him forget how sinful it could be.

For Zig, this was an impulse, a temptation that he could not stop himself from indulging. It was the first time that he realized that his drawings meant something vital to the people that were dreaming them. Later he learned that it was the work of an Oracle reader, which broke all the Sanescidian rules. A slave doing something that only the noblest of citizens were allowed do, worse, only those chosen by the Gods were allowed to do. It was preposterous, unacceptable. When his owner was caught, they both got the death sentence. Zig should have died in a most humiliating way, and he almost did, but he was saved by an Oksaleb attack. The ship with the incandescent light had extracted him from the rubble and had revived him. From then on, he had been strictly following the Oracle's advice and he knew that that was why he was still alive in this new world and not a dead slave in the old one.

The day before, he had not followed the Oracle. He had attended the party Jeannie had lured him to, exhausted from dealing with patrons asking questions for which he had no answers to give. He had left the gallery early for his hotel and fallen asleep. Jeannie had woken him up and pushed him to the party. "You'll get to know people your age with your interests, love!"

Why would yesterday be different? he thought. But he just felt that it was. Finding nothing, he felt a great emptiness. He started scavenging in the recycling bin beside the table, grateful that no one had taken it out yet. Otherwise he could easily imagine himself diving into the commercial bin on the street.

"Vat the hell are you doing now!" yelled Brenne, running to grab him.

Zig came out clutching all the notes and started to read them one by one. One had been ripped into pieces. He picked out as many of the pieces as he could find and tried to put them together, managing to make a piece of a sentence: *...make you suc...* Then underneath: *... won't be eas...* He looked at the assistant curator. "You think this one was for Rosy?"

Rosy was one of the young artists that came to the gallery even less than Zig. She had been fighting Brenne since the first day and definitely was not interested in doing a better job. Actually, she hadn't been seen for a while.

Brenne had a murderous expression—tunnel sight, crooked mouth—but he did not move nor did he answer. By then a few of the artists were surrounding Zig and all seemed interested in helping him find whatever he was looking for. Some of them were already scavenging in the other recycling bins, either helping Zig's search or maybe looking for messages for themselves. "Why on earth does Brenne throw away anything that's not a business card? He has such lack of respect towards us! We fucking pay his salary!" murmured someone.

"I'm going to complain to the president," said Nick, one of the most well-known artists. "Who's coming with me?"

All agreed to go, but they would have to wait for the end of the day.

"Hey, Zig, I found an envelope with your name here!" It was Nick, again. Zig had heard that he was also a very famous architect. "It actually says: 'For Zigor.' Is that you?"

Zig paled. Nobody in this world knew that name. True, Zig and Zigor were similar, but still. He nodded and thanked Nick. He opened the envelope and unfolded the note. Everybody was watching.

Dear Zigor,

I find your work outstanding! I would love to have met you yesterday, but you were already gone. I'm not a professional artist, nor a critic, but I need to talk to you about your work. If you decide not to meet me, or this note doesn't reach you, I wish you the best with all my heart and I'll pray for you every day of my life.

In case you do want to meet me, I'm staying at the Platzel Hotel till Sunday morning. My phone number is......................
If there's no chance of meeting me here, my cellphone number at home, in Canada is ....
Yours, Aileen Blight.

He folded it and put it in his pocket. Could it be the lady he was supposed to meet? If so, he still had a chance. As he turned to go to the artists' room he bumped into Brenne.

"I'm very sorry for having been so irresponsible, sir. This won't happen again, I promise. By the way, have you heard from Rosy?"

Brenne couldn't believe the change of attitude Zig was having, but he was not going to lift his hopes of him yet. He turned around to leave. "Where is Rosy, indeed," he muttered, and bumped into Jeannie.

"How dare you treat an ARTIST like THIS! You'll hear from us." she said.

"No, we won't, sir," reassured Zig. Then he looked at Jeannie and shook his head.

"What's going on, Zig?" she said.

"Nothing is going on, Miss Wells, except that I don't need your services anymore."

"And why is that?"

"Because you lead me away from the path I need to take! You invite me to all those useless parties, you decide for me, and that cannot happen any longer."

"What the hell are you talking about!?" She was mad.

"You've tried to get me off track 'cause you don't want me to follow..." Shit, he almost messed up. "You've pushed me to be irresponsible. You know well enough."

"You're the one that gets drunk and acts reckless!" she shot

15

back. When he didn't answer, she said desperately, "You can't do that!" But she knew he could. By then, he knew how to deal in *Etwo* (Earth in their language). He was a fast learner and he had the means. She had nothing more to teach him.

He turned around and went to the artists' room. By then, all the other artists had gone. It was time to prepare.

Meanwhile, Jeannie was standing dumbfounded. What had just happened? Was she really fired? Why was Zig so emotional? She couldn't understand it, so she decided that she would give him some space. She was sure that he would need her sooner or later. In a week or so, he would call her, or else she'd have to call Central Operations. She had no idea at that moment that she was not going to see Zig for a long time.

Zig took the folded paper from his pocket. Aileen Blight. He closed his eyes, trying to picture the woman he'd seen in the prophetic dream and compare her with the name. "Just because she wrote my complete name doesn't mean that she's the one," he thought. "Zigor is a Basque name in this world." On the other hand, if she had been the one he'd been looking for...No matter how shy he was, he was going to have to call her. He was very upset with himself. "Why did I let Jeannie decide for me when I already had commitments?" he thought. Then he remembered what she had said, "This party is an opportunity for your future, sugar! You need to join *la crème de la crème*. You are too good to be working for free in that stupid museum." She went on and on. He wasn't better than any of these artists. They were all outstanding, especially Vivienne, and Nick's sculptures! All of the participants were better than him and definitely more professional. He understood Brenne's hatred. *Where does this irresponsible amateur come from, taking away someone else's chance to this incredible experience?* He was right.

Now, Zig had probably missed the chance to see in person the woman he needed to meet, according to the Oracle. He was hoping to get a second chance.

* * *

Vivienne, one of the more famous young artists, and Stephan invited Zig for lunch for the first time since the exhibition had begun. He accepted. It was a good opportunity to get to know them better. No one had gotten even near him until that day and he wondered if it had to do with the fact that he was alone for the first time. He'd always been with Jeannie before. Three whole weeks already, his last day in the museum, and only now a few of the artists wanted to meet him.

They joined Nick, who was reading a book alone at the cafeteria.

"Vat are you reading?" asked Vivienne, very interested. She seemed interested in anything to do with Nick. It made sense. He was very attractive, bright, and creative.

He showed her—it was a book about the most amazing buildings. He began to show her the work of an architect he admired, whose name Zig did not catch. Stephan also joined the conversation. Zig could only listen. He had no idea who the people they were talking about were.

"So, Zig..." Stephan interrupted his thoughts. "Where did you study art?"

He seems condescending, Zig thought. *He probably doesn't like my stuff, just like Brenne.* "Just practiced on my own," he said. "How 'bout you?"

"Are you telling me that you've never been to art school?" Stephan exclaimed. "How is it that you are here?" He was shocked, unable to believe how this kid, with no real artistic education, was exhibiting such good work. How did they find him? Was he a fraud? "How do I know that those pictures are yours?"

"Cool down, man," said Nick, coming to Zig's rescue, "He's just a genius, so what? What's your problem? You got up on the wrong side of the bed, or what?"

"Sorry," said Stephan. "I just can't believe that this brat's so good."

Zig got up and left, leaving his food behind. He was embarrassed. He knew he didn't belong among these artists who had so much education. He only recently had learned to read and write and do basic math. He was a nobody, he himself couldn't believe that he'd managed to get this amazing opportunity, among the best Surrealist artists. It was a miracle. Stephan was right to be angry because Zig did think of himself a phony. All the other exhibiting artists were obviously better. He knew that he had gotten in only because the gods of the Oracle had helped. It had been a bad idea to have lunch with the others.

"Hey, Zig, not so fast!" he heard Nick call behind him. He turned around and saw him balancing two trays. "Let me join you wherever you are going, so my question is, where to?"

Zig was really embarrassed now. "Sorry Nick," he said, "I lost my appetite. I'm heading back to the office."

"No, man. Please let me join you! Stephan is a jerk. He's not worth it. Let's sit on that bench. It's a beautiful day!" Vivienne was approaching with her lunch tray, too, agreeing what a great place the cold and maybe wet stone bench that Nick was referring to was.

Zig reluctantly agreed, grabbed his tray from Nick, and the

three of them sat on the bench. It was indeed cold, but luckily not wet.

"Dumbass Korbes is jealous," said Nick.

"Why?" said Zig, "All of you are way better than me. Why would he be jealous?"

"Because his stuff is empty. Not like yours," said Nick. "Your work, little man, is the real thing."

"I totally agree!" said Vivienne. "Little man?" She looked at Nick, puzzled. "Zat's a funny name for a guy his size, ha ha!" Zig was near six feet tall, though skinny.

Zig understood why Nick was calling him 'little man.' He was probably only 18 (having been a slave for so long and barely remembering his life at the *Gaztello* he had no idea how old he really was), when the youngest of them was around thirty. But he didn't understand what they meant by his stuff being the real thing. "What do you mean?" he asked. "Stephan's art is incredible compared to mine, and yours," he added, now looking at Vivienne, "is the best thing I've ever seen." Then he turned to Nick, "That is, the best thing not counting your sculptures, Nick! You are teasing me, aren't you?"

"No, Zig. We are serious. Your work is outstanding. It has soul. It's full of meaning that doesn't need interpreting. That's why Stephan is so angry, but he has no right to be. Whether you studied here or there doesn't make who you are."

Vivienne was nodding. "By ze way, vhere are you from?" she said. "You don't seem American, or are you?"

"No. I'm supposed to be from some place in Spain or France," he invented, "but I was abducted when I was a baby and was something like a slave. I never went to school, but I started to do my drawings in hiding, in the little free time I had from work, until someone found out." He saw the shocked faces of

Vivienne and Nick, and turned bright red. "Sorry!" was all he could think to say.

Vivienne gave him a big hug and said, "Zig, you did go to a school of art, and maybe one of the best ones! Please count on me always, ok?" She noticed that he didn't want to talk about himself and she wasn't sure she wanted to know more, either. Sometimes we are not prepared to listen to other people's horror stories.

"Ok," Zig said, reading her mind. She was right. He didn't want to talk about his pathetic past life either, much less to someone like her, who seemed perfect, especially when he had to modify it so much.

"Same here, little man, always count on me," said Nick. "I think you and I are similar souls. Now, let's eat."

By the end of the day, Zig felt exhausted, but for the first time, happy. This was his last day, the only day he'd done a good job. He had talked to everyone that wanted to talk with him and ask questions and, most important, had been polite and genuinely interested in the patrons' questions. Stephan had been right when he'd called him a brat. No matter his history, he had acted like one. On the other hand, he was very thankful for the opportunity Vivienne and Nick had given him. He was wondering whether he was going to see them again.

Brenne was approaching. "Mr. Sanescid!"

"Mr. Brenne," said Zig, "I thank you for the opportunity you gave me to be here. I wish..."

"Did you know that your work was voted the best, the most innovative, et cetera, et cetera, among the public, no matter your bad manners?" His praise sounded more insulting than congratulatory.

Zig had had no idea and turned red yet again. "I don't think

I deserve it," he said, and turned around to continue packing his things.

"You don't understand, Mr. Sanescid. This means that the public will want you to stay one more week." Brenne said this with a sour face, as if it was a huge sacrifice to deal with this young and irresponsible man for one more week.

"Mr. Brenne," said Zig, leaving what he was doing and looking the man straight in the eye, actually startling him. "You are not the only one that has had a horrible week. I've had it just as bad dealing with you, sir. You are among the most disagreeable persons I've ever met and trust me, I used to live in hell. I thank you for the news you just gave me, though I've never cared about what people think of what I do because I've never expected to be praised. About staying one more week, I can't, not because I can't physically stay, but because I don't want to."

Zig turned back around and continued to pack. He couldn't stand to be around the assistant curator one day longer. It was true that he had played a part in this disagreeable relationship, but he couldn't stop himself.

Nick had been at the door, wanting to invite Zig out, and had heard the conversation. The door was open, so anybody could have heard it. "Good evening Mr. Brenne," he said. "I'd like a word with you later." Then he turned to Zig, without waiting for an answer. "Hey, man, are you up to celebrating?"

Zig wasn't. "No, I have nothing to celebrate. Hey! You called me man and not little man!" he exclaimed, smiling.

"See? That's what we're celebrating. Your smile."

"Thanks, but no," said Zig. "I don't behave well at parties. I get too stressed, then I begin to drink. I'm not nice." He was planning to get drunk, but alone.

21

"Zig," Nick said, "this celebration will be only for us: you, me... Anybody else you'd like to invite?"

"No stranger whom I have to smile for?"

"No stranger whom you have to smile for," said Nick.

"Just like lunch, but without Stephan?"

"Without Stephan, and with whoever else you'd like to invite."

"Let me reach someone on the phone first, ok?"

"Sure, man. Do you want a ride to your hotel?" said Nick. "Seems you got a lot of stuff to take back."

"Aren't you having to take yours back?" Nick would have a much harder job taking care of his sculptures, thought Zig.

"Nah. I'll leave them for one more week and then I have a team that takes care of that part."

Nick helped Zig with his work, and then he helped him move from his old hotel to the Platzel, where Zig had already booked the simplest room available. To him the simplest room in one of these hotels was still utter luxury after having lived his whole life sleeping on the ground, outdoors, huddled with the other slaves to keep warm, like working animals, or worse. Only now, after more than a year, was he getting used to this luxury.

When picking up his things, which were very few, at the former hotel, he found a message from Jeannie. *When you stop acting out, give me a call.* He threw it in the waste basket. Then he grabbed his phone, placed it on the floor, and stepped on it, making sure it was completely broken.

Nick raised his eyebrows but said nothing.

Once Zig was settled in his new room, Nick left, promising to pick him up in an hour. Zig was still nervous about it, but had decided, *What the heck?* Worst-case scenario he could leave the group any time he wanted. The room had a double bed, a desk, and a chair. On one side of the bed, by the side table, there was an armchair; in front there was a dresser with a little fridge beside it. On top of the fridge there was a coffeemaker with coffee, tea, and chocolate sachets on one side, and creamer, sugar, and aspartame envelopes on the other. The room looked modern, though very simple.

* * *

As Nick had promised, Zig had fun for the first time. Vivienne, Nick, and he went to a nearby pub and ordered food and beer. Another of the artists, Jean Pierre, walked in to meet another group of friends, saw them, and called over a greeting. "Ey! Good to see you! So, the champions celebrate together?"

Nick and Vivienne stood up to salute. Zig felt compelled to stand too, but was afraid to receive an insult, like he had from Stephan. Instead, Jean Pierre came straight over to him and gave him a strong hug. *"Mon Dieu, ton travail est formidable! Félicitations, mon ami!"* Then he gave a hug to Vivienne. "Obvious that you were going to win, *ma cherie*, outstanding as ever!" Then he gave her a kiss on each cheek. Vivienne responded in kind. Finally, he gave a big hug to Nick.

"No kiss for me, Jean?" said Nick.

"Not my type, *monsieur*." They all laughed. "So," he said, looking at Zig.

"Please don't ask me what fucking school I come from." Zig tensed.

"How does it feel to be so young and famous?" Jean Pierre said instead. "And by the way, aren't you guys supposed to be at the champions' reception?"

Zig had no idea what Jean Pierre was talking about. If there was an invitation, he clearly hadn't gotten it.

"Nah, said Nick. "We wanted to celebrate on our own."

The people that were waiting for Jean Pierre were intrigued about what was taking him so long, and one of them approached the group. "So, what's up?" he said.

"Look here, Paul," Jean Pierre said, "these are the winners of the Surrealist exhibition, and since they are who they are, they are here celebrating instead of at the ceremony! Why don't we grab another table and sit with them?"

Paul called to the rest of his friends sitting on the far side of the bar and dragged a table over with the help of Jean Pierre.

3

His Voice

Aileen and Ulrich were exhausted but pleased. First, they'd been to the gorgeous Schloss Nymphenburg and admired its extraordinary beauty. At around 1pm, they had lunch at a café and walked towards the Marienplatz. They took in the square by the Mariensäule column, with the golden Virgin Mary on the top and the historic buildings surrounding it. They walked by the stores and saw the most amazing woodcraft. *Almost magical*, thought Aileen. She always wondered at the level of perfection humans could reach. The Renaissance was definitely a special period for focusing on beauty and perfection, following the Medieval Age when God was the center of everything. In the Renaissance, man was the center. God had been set aside, for civilization was harking back to Greek philosophy, beauty, and style.

They sat at a *biergarten* and tasted the local beer alongside a very appetizing sandwich. Then, they walked to the English Garden, their next planned destination because they had heard very good comments about the place, and it was on the way back to the hotel. They walked across the park until their legs started to complain.

"Time to head home," said Ulrich, and Aileen agreed gladly.

In the room, Ulrich noticed a light on the phone. He listened to the message and realized it was for Aileen.

"Hello, Mrs. Blight," it said. "I'm Zigor." The name was emphasized. "We can meet tomorrow at your hotel at 10 for breakfast. Hope to see you." Click.

His voice! She had never heard Zigor talk in her dream. She'd heard him sobbing silently and screaming in pain. Was this the same Zigor? She'd written his name on purpose, to see if there was a response, and there it was. His name was Zigor, and the pictures in the museum were definitely those of her dreams, but in her dreams, she had drawn the first one, and had imagined the other ones. Finally, if the place of her dreams really existed, where was it? There was nothing even similar to it anywhere around the world. She had been doing research because she had been looking for these children. It had felt like something urgent. After getting nowhere for so long, she had given up and had decided it was her imagination. Until now.

"Breakfast at 10. Uh-huh," said Ulrich. "Did he leave a phone number? We'll waste a lot of time if we wait till 10am!"

Aileen agreed, but her legs were hurting. "Maybe it's a good idea to take it easy tomorrow," she said. "After all, we are not that young any more, are we? My legs ache."

"I guess I can get some work done, too," said Ulrich, and so it was agreed.

4

Nick the Xanaduan

Nick suddenly saw him. The stranger was looking at him, unblinking. He had a mark similar to Zig's. *An Ewan (the planet where Jeanny, and the other caretaker come from, as well as Zigor and, what the Ethrean called Oksalebs)*, thought Nick. The man was outside the café-restaurant, standing still with his eyes on Nick. "Hey Zig," he said. "Do you know that man? He's been watching us for a while."

Zig turned around and saw the stranger. He stood and walked outside, towards the man, "What do you want?" he said.

"Where's Jeannie, Mr. Sanescid?"

"I don't know, and I don't care," Zig replied. The moment he'd gotten rid of her he'd met all these people and had fit right in. "Look, I'm not even drunk! So, I ask again. What do you want?"

"We can't leave you alone, you know that. What would happen to us if you disappear, if you got abducted again by those bastards?" the man said, looking at Nick again. "What do you think will happen?"

Zig half believed the abduction story. Even though he had a hard time trying to get information from his rescuers, the only thing he had clear was that he was an important person to Ewan, but he couldn't understand why. He knew that he belonged to these people because all had a mark like his, by the right eye. The only difference was the design. The same mark that had cursed him in Ethrea was expected in Ewan. He also knew they could read his mind, just like he could read theirs most of the time, but he couldn't understand the way they acted. They were totally alien to him. *Gods*, he felt more at home on this planet called Earth by its citizens (or Etwo by Ewans) than with the people looking after him. It didn't mean that he didn't appreciate all they had done for him, saving him from slavery and inminent death in Ethrea. But he felt overwhelmed with somebody all the time on his heels.

"I'm having fun, for the first time. Why can't you leave me be?"

"I will," said the man, "but I'll watch you at a distance. Please understand that it's for your own good." He passed him a weird-looking cell phone, while still watching Nick, making Zig look too.

"Goodbye," Zig said, placing the phone in his pocket, still not sure what to do with it.

Nick was uneasy about the stranger but tried not to show it. He feigned paying attention to Jean Pierre, who was describing a funny story that had happened to Brenne and himself.

"But Mr. Sola! Vat is that?" he was saying. "It's a penne Mr. Brenne. P-e-n-n-e." And he was so serious, *mon Dieu!*"

They were all laughing when Zig came back. Zig realized that he was feeling tired. Every time he had a nightmare, he felt tired all day, as if he hadn't slept at all. It was already 11pm. "I think I'm heading home," he said.

"I can give you a ride. I'm tired too, man," said Nick.

As they were approaching Nick's car, Nick felt someone behind him and a gun at his head. No one except for Zig seemed to be in the parking lot at that moment.

"What are you?" said the stranger who had been checking on Zig before.

"What the…?" said Zig.

"ANSWER!"

"I'm Nicholas Xenium," Nick said, calmly, though he was in fear for his life.

"Xanaduan. I knew it! I should kill you right here and now," the man said in a lower voice. *Hadn't a Xenium killed Rick King, who was supposed to be their natural governor?* he thought.

"I don't think it's a good idea," Nick said, maintaining his calm. "I'm very famous around this world, and I have many friends. Some very powerful, even for you."

Xanaduan? thought Zig, feeling the blood go up to his face as an uncontrollable rage began to take hold of him. Weren't they the ones who had kidnapped his ancestors and were suspected of kidnapping him, too?

He struck Nick straight on the face so hard that Nick fell to the floor, bumping his head on the sidewalk and losing consciousness for a few seconds. As he came back, Zig was on him, choking him. Nick let him go for it, not fighting back. The stranger was trying to intervene, "Don't Zig! He's right! Here's too dangerous and we might get in trouble. Help me get him into the car!"

Zig saw Nick's very pale face, blood running from his nose, which seemed twisted to the right, and let go. "Why did you do that to me? I'm all fucked up, forever. Was that why? Why the fuck were you so friendly? You want to take me back? Don't you fucking know that Sanescid doesn't even exist anymore?"

Nick could only see red in Zig's eyes. "I don't know what you are talking about," he said as he tried to take in air. He breathed through his mouth, as his nose kept on bleeding and his face was beginning to swell. He shook his head.

"I thought you were my friend," sobbed Zig.

"Me too," gasped Nick.

"But you are Xanaduan!"

"Not my fault."

"Don't listen to him," said the man, "He's trying to…"

"SHUT UP!" said Zig. "Take us to the Platze Hotel!"

They took the stranger's car. Zig picked up Nick, bundled him into the back seat, and climbed in beside him. "My people…" It still sounded strange to call them so. "They told me that your people abducted me. Is it true?"

"My people," said Nick with difficulty, "are horrible people… and could have abducted you… as your people… have told you… but I have no idea. See? I'm an outcast… That's why I'm here."

"Why are you interested in me?" asked Zig.

"I like you… I like your art."

They were arriving at the hotel. The man parked. "I'll take care of this." He pointed to Nick.

Zig didn't know what to do. There was a lot of blood on Nick's face. He had probably broken his nose, and he was breathing with difficulty. "No," he said. "Nick is innocent. Don't touch him!" He remembered how awful he had felt at the museum cafeteria until Nick had helped him. How Nick had defended him, first from Stephan, then Brenne. Tonight

30

he had had the best time ever. Now, just because Nick was Xanaduan, they were about to kill him? "You, the one that belongs to 'my people'," he said, looking at the man, "you people always manage to make me miserable!" Tears were about to spring from his eyes. "First Jeannie with her outstanding way of doing what she wants because that's what's supposed to be good for me, and now you, a man with no name because you won't even fucking tell it to me"—*probably doesn't want to get attached to me*, thought Zig bitterly—"are about to kill the only person that has made me feel human! Get the fuck out! I don't want your help. GET OUT OF MY LIFE!"

A very strange car had just parked beside them. A man who looked to be in his forties got out, a Ewan gun pointing to the stranger as he stepped out of the car. "Pass me the Xanaduan, Oksaleb."

The man turned to look and could not believe what he was seeing. It was the King himself. What could that mean?

"Five, four, three…" he said, warningly.

"A King Ramos," the man said.

"…two, one…"

"What is a King Ramos doing with a Xanaduan?"

Zap. The man disappeared.

"What the fuck?" said Zig.

"You're next. I repeat, pass me the Xanaduan."

Zig was shocked, but, even though he had been beating on Nick not long before, now he wanted to protect him. He asked Nick, "You ok with this man?" He was not willing to let Nick go if he didn't want to, no matter what the consequences.

Nick smiled, though it looked more like a grimace, and said, "I told you guys to leave me alone, that I had very important people covering my back. Let me introduce you to my master,

31

David King.'

"Master?" What the heck was going on?

"He told you he was an outcast," said King. "Master, for him, doesn't mean the same as here on Earth. Now hand him over to me or I'll shoot. Five, four…"

Nick moved to King's side and started to apologize. "Sorry I made you come," which sounded more like "Zowy I bade u cub." David looked at Nick's face and touched it very delicately to see whether there were more bones broken, other than the nose. "Get in the car. We must act as fast as we can if you really want to continue participating in the exhibition, or have you lost interest?"

Nick was trying to say something, but David stopped him. "Don't say anything. Just lie down and relax." Very carefully, David strapped Nick into the passenger seat. Then he closed the door and went to the back. "So that kiddo, the one who broke your nose and tried to choke you, is the reason you don't want to continue at the museum?… Because they treated the brat badly? Sorry, Nick. I have no sympathy for someone that tries to kill an innocent person just because he's from Xanadu… Ah, so he changed his mind, but after beating you!… Sorry. I can't feel sympathy… I won't let you put the guilt on yourself… As you were saying before… who do you respond to?… Aha, that's better."

For anyone watching and listening he looked like a crazy person or a drug addict, but Zig figured out that this Mr. King was from Ewan, and that he was actually talking while reading Nick's mind, to prevent him from opening his mouth and save him the pain. He also noticed that he didn't have a mark, which was odd.

"What the heck are you still doing here?" David said, now

looking at Zig.

"I'm sorry!" And he was, *Gods* he was. He turned around to leave.

"What?"

Zig turned back to repeat what he had said, but saw that King was looking at Nick. He turned around and headed to the hotel. This time he'd really messed up.

"Hey kiddo!" he heard King call. He turned around, ready for more insults. "So, you are supposed to be the lost Oksaleb kid? That's what Nick is telling me. Come in here so we can chat. Promise I won't bite." He waved an inviting hand at the car.

The car looked strange from the outside, a brand Zig had never seen before, but still looked like a regular size car, though fancy. Inside was something else. It reminded Zig of Doctor Who's Tardis, but not so dramatic. Inside it seemed more spacious. The seat where Nick was lying looked more like a bed from a clinic; actually, Zig noticed that all the space looked like a clinic. Nick already had a mask on his face that seemed to be moving underneath. His eyes were closed.

"Yeah," said King as if Zig had asked a question, "the mask is fixing the fracture you made. He will still be very bruised, but he'll be able to go to work, if he wants to."

"So sorr…"

"What's your name?" interrupted King.

"Zigor Sanescid."

"That doesn't sound Oksaleb. Probably not your real name. Now, why do they think you are that one lost kid? And why would the Xanaduans do it? Unless hired by someone interested in making you disappear?"

Zig felt lonelier than ever. "I don't know, sir," he said. This

Mr. King was right. What if the ones that were taking care of him were the same as the ones that had made him disappear in the first place? Who could he really trust?

"I'll send your man back. His name's Renith. I believe you can trust him. Nick is also nagging me to give you this." He held out a phone as weird as the one Renith had given Zig earlier. "In case you need him, press here," he said. "Now, goodbye." He turned around to continue taking care of Nick.

Zig lingered, looking at Nick's mask, then murmured, "I'm very sorry, Nick," and left.

He walked to the lobby, then decided to take the stairs. What had he done? Xanaduans were supposed to be the *cucos* of their world, the worst monsters in the universe! Except that Nick was the contrary. Zig had met the very first Xanaduan who had been a good man, who had made him feel valuable, and he had broken his nose and strangled him in gratitude. For the very first time he had felt that he belonged, and he had fucked up. Damn, he was a piece of work.

He opened the door, took a shower, and headed to bed. He did not think capable of sleeping that night as guilt penetrated in all his pores.

5

The Meeting

"*Hello, John.*"

"*David, little bro! What a miracle! What's up?*"

"*Just met your lost—and now found—grandchild. Why didn't you tell me?*"

"*Our family used you too long for babysitting. I didn't want to bother you. Now that you know, though...*"

"*I'll check on him from afar,*" said David.

"*Thanks, bro. Always love you.*"

"*Me too. But I wasn't babysitting. It was my own brother!*"

"*I know, but we should have been more by your side, little bro.*"

The child was manacled beside other children. They were all sleeping. Some seemed to be having bad dreams, but none seemed to be awake. A big man, his keys jangling on his waist, approached to unlock the child's manacles. The child woke up and began to scream, waking the others. Huge eyes were now observing how the man slapped the little boy hard and put a balled-up cloth in his mouth.

"Hush, you bastards! If you say anything, I'll burn you alive," he told the rest as he tied the child and put him in a sack as

35

one would do a sheep. The child was fighting with all he had, kicking and squirming, but to no avail.

She was a mere spectator, like a ghost. She tried so hard to help the poor child in any way. Suddenly she was woken by screams, seeping through from the waking world. They were not a child's screams, but those of a man. It sounded so terrible that she got up and out of the room, to check the rooms beside and across from hers; she scanned the doors, wondering where the noise had come from. She heard someone, maybe sobbing? It sounded muffled, as if through a pillow. Maybe someone was choking this man with a pillow! She began to freak out, but then there was total silence. Had it been real or her imagination? She was so used to reading mysteries and watching them on TV that she began to doubt if it had really happened. She wasn't sure which door the noise had come from, if there had even been one, so she stayed a little longer to listen. The place was in complete silence. She walked by the doors she thought the muffled sound could have come from but heard nothing. She put her ear against one door. No sound. Then she tried the next one, then the one opposite to hers. Had she imagined it all? Had the scream just come from the nightmare she'd awakened from? She had been ready to call the police, but now she wasn't sure. She went back to bed. Ulrich seemed to be sleeping soundly. That convinced her that everything, including the man's screams, had been part of the dream. *Nobody could keep sleeping as if nothing had happened after a scream like that*, she thought.

Morning came fast. Aileen woke up exhausted, as if she hadn't slept at all. She looked at the clock: 8am. "Oh my God, so late!" She scurried out of bed and into the shower. It wasn't that they had anything to do—after all, they had decided to take it easy that day—but she still felt bad about staying in bed so late. They hadn't decided yet whether she was going to meet Zigor alone or they would go together. Once showered and dressed, she went down for breakfast. She hadn't seen her husband yet, though she hoped to see him in the lobby or the restaurant.

Ulrich was at the restaurant with a glass of juice and an empty plate that looked like it might have once contained scrambled eggs. He was immersed in a book. He looked up as Aileen approached. "Hey! How did you sleep?"

"Awful! I had a nightmare that woke me up in the middle of the night, then I thought I heard someone scream, so I went outside to check," she said. "Did you hear anything?"

"No, not a thing," he said.

"I figured. It must have been my imagination or the dream. Then, I had a really hard time getting back to sleep. How about you? You slept well?"

"Like a log, until I woke up at four. Do you think something happened in one of the rooms?"

"I hope not. Have you seen anything different or heard any comment about something happening last night?"

"No," he said. "So, what was the nightmare about?"

She told him. She told him how she had been a mere spectator and how frustrating it had been not being able to help that little creature, and how real the dream seemed, like the ones she had had all those years before. Just as she had feared, they were coming back. The worst bit of all was how real the man's scream had been when she thought herself awake. "I thought someone was being murdered! But when I saw you sleeping so placidly, I realized that the sound must have been part of my dream." She couldn't imagine anybody being able

37

to keep on sleeping after that haunted scream.

"So, it was one of those strange dreams like you had seven years ago?"

"Yes," she said. "The boy being abducted might have been the same little one I'd dreamed about back then."

"Hmm," he said, "I hope that they aren't coming back. You suffered too much. And the headaches!"

"I know!" She was upset. "Well, I'm going to grab something for breakfast."

"I'll be in the lobby, if you need me, unless you want me to go with you?"

"It's ok, love. I should go alone."

* * *

Zig opened his eyes to see the time staring at him accusingly: 9:30. He forgot to set the alarm. Oh gods! He'd slept like crap. First the horrible nightmare; then, he woke up and realized that he was screaming in a room surrounded by other rooms full of strangers, where Jeannie wasn't around to calm him down as she used to. He only hoped that nobody had heard him. At least the pillow seemed to help muffle the sound. He'd stayed awake for a long time, trembling and breathing shallowly, until he had finally fallen back asleep, but it hadn't been restful at all. He felt as if a truck had run over him, a mix of heaviness and emptiness.

Then he remembered what he had done the night before. Goodbye Nick's friendship, and Vivienne's! Even though she hadn't been there last night, she would eventually find out. She was probably not going to be interested in being his friend after what he'd done. "Damn me!" he thought.

The man, who he knew now was called Renith, had never been interested in being friends with him. He had been assigned to look after him; a bodyguard. It was just a job: to keep him alive and out of trouble. For the gods' sake, he hadn't even told him his name for a whole year! He had clearly not been interested in creating any bond. Zig felt miserable.

He suddenly remembered that he was going to meet the lady that had written to him, at 10am. He hoped that it was the one the Oracle had mentioned. It was 9:45 already, and he needed a shower desperately. Suddenly he heard a knock on the door. "Who is it?" Maybe someone from the hotel to complain about the noise last night, the scream.

"It's me, sir." It was Renith.

"Say your name!" He was not letting him in otherwise.

"Renith, sir."

Zig opened the door. Renith stepped in and bowed in front of Zig. "I'm very sorry, sir. I was wrong, but I was trying to keep you safe, I swear!"

Zigor was surprised. "Why do you bow?" As a former slave, he had to be more in that position—kneeling and subservient—than not and he had hated it very much. "Never do that in front of me, please!"

"Please forgive me first. I promise to never do it again, but I need your forgiveness first."

Or else what? wondered Zig. "I understand that you were trying to do your job," he said. "I don't think you have had too many cases like me in your career, have you?"

"No, sir, it's my first one. There was a similar case many years ago. The King-Ramos family had lost a newborn. I think it was at least forty years ago now. The person you met last night was the twin brother. I was told to not give you my name, so that you didn't get fond of me.

Or him of me, thought Zig.

"I've gotten worried about losing you, especially when you go wandering around, not wanting any company, or befriending people when I can't figure out if they are good or bad. Then, there was that Xanaduan!"

"Had you ever met one before, Renith?"

"Never, but I'd been hearing terrible stories about them since I was a little child. They were the ones who had abducted Sir Rick King, Dr. David's twin brother, when he was a newborn. As a security guard, I was taught to shoot them to kill. I had no idea that any of them could be a good person. By law, they are supposed to stay where they belong, which is Xanadu. I don't think that Dr. King is doing something legal, but it's not my business. I never imagined that you could befriend one before befriending even a human!" he said.

"I've got to meet someone in the restaurant and I'm running late," said Zig. "While I'm there, please go to reception and ask for a change of room. Ask them if they have a penthouse with at least two rooms, preferably." He wanted to be able to scream as loud as he had to when having any of his horrible nightmares without worrying anyone. The nightmares were not going to go away any time soon, so he had to be able to be in control when they came. "Gods, it's getting late!" He ran for the shower.

* * *

At the restaurant, he scanned the people sitting at tables: a couple with two children, two elderly people, probably in their seventies, a group of seven young people about his age laughing carelessly. He wondered if he had looked like that the night before, having so much fun at the pub... And there was a woman, probably in her fifties, reading an ebook. The table had had food for two, so he decided that it wasn't her. He went to the buffet and chose scrambled eggs, toast, fruit, and a coffee, no milk, no sugar. He should have brought something to read. He looked around and found a pile of newspapers in German, French, and English, one from England and *The New York Times*. He picked this one up. He scanned the place again, and then sat down with the newspaper. Nobody was looking at him, so he opened it and started browsing.

Aileen had gotten so focused on her reading that she didn't notice when Zig entered the restaurant. She was looking straight ahead in deep thought when she saw him. "Zigor, oh God!'" He was the young man she'd dreamed, just a little older, but the same person! Now she was scared to approach him. *What was I thinking!* She wished she could disappear. She began to invent excuses for herself. *It's not important to meet him; he seems to be doing great; what am I going to tell him? Why on earth...?* But she had to meet him. It wasn't necessary to make a fuss, just tell him about the paintings. He must have needed to see her too, otherwise he wouldn't have called her back. *Do it for him.* She walked over to where he sat.

"Hi," she said.

He looked up. So that was Mrs. Blight, the woman that had been reading the ebook. "Hello," he said. For some reason, he felt that he had seen her before, which didn't make sense.

"May I sit?"

"Please," he said with a wary, thin smile.

"I'm Aileen Blight." She extended her hand to him.

He kept on looking at her, scrutinizing her. Then he

41

extended his hand in return. "I understand that you wanted to talk with me about my art?" he said.

"Yes! By the way, you are outstanding. Congratulations!"

"Thank you." He waited.

"I don't know how to start. A few years ago, I began to have strange dreams…" And she told him about one of the first ones, the one where she had dreamed about the Oracle, and inside the dream, how she'd woken up with the painting in front of her and how her hands were dirty. So, she had imagined that she had painted it.

"How long ago did you dream this?" he said. His voice was soft and low.

"About seven years ago," she said.

Why? he wondered. He was looking absentmindedly at the scrambled eggs as he steered them around with the fork. The only possible connection was that around that time he had started to paint stuff that he had been dreaming about.

"In the dream, I—I'm something like a queen of a place named Sanescid. They call me Anier," she said.

He stopped stirring and put his hands down. Then he looked at her with unhidden hate. "We're done, Mrs. whatever your name is," he said. "I don't care if you think my paintings are my own or some bitch that abandoned her kid to slavery drew them. Try to prove it if you want." He stood and left.

Aileen had no idea what had just happened. She'd never accused him of anything! She only wanted to understand why one of his pictures was the same as the one she'd made in her dream. She also had thought that, somehow, she could be of help, but how? Why the hell had she wanted to meet him if not for mere curiosity? Maybe it had been pure selfishness.

She felt all her guts tighten up and a chill passed through her body. She stood and hurriedly took the elevator for her room. Tears started to come and she began to shake. Luckily, she didn't meet anyone on her way. It had all been so random, from the first dreams seven years ago till now, when a young man looking exactly like the one she had seen in the market when M'Anier had died had just left without eating his breakfast, and hated her. She felt so guilty, as if she had really been that queen, his mother. But that was in her dreams, for God's sake! It was not real! How on earth was he here, then? What was the connection between her and Zigor? Clearly, he had wanted to meet her. Not any more, from the moment she told him who she'd been in the dreams.

"Oh!" she said to herself. "Why am I so ridiculous?" She ran to her bed and let herself cry out the embarrassment. Then she went to the bathroom and washed her face. As she looked at herself in the mirror, she remembered that after her meeting with the kid, she was going to join Ulrich in the lobby. Now she wanted to walk around the city. Walking would help her forget what had happened, she hoped. Then, they should leave Munich. It was time to leave.

6

A Confusing Oracle

He was furious. **She was M'Anier in her dreams? The horrible woman who had never** wanted to see him from the moment he and his brother had been born? He had dreamed the paintings! They were his! He had dreamed and painted them as he had seen them in his dreams.

He had dreamed so many Oracle dreams belonging to others, had painted them and given them to his master, but these particular dreams belonged to him and his brother! He could even see the meaning of them.

Who was this woman? Why did the Oracle want him to meet her? Fuck it. He didn't want to see her ever again. Not even if he ended up in hell. He had been most of his life there anyway. Sadly, he had been getting soft since his rescue and so now he feared going back again. He was ready to die, but before that, he would fight if necessary. No matter what the future was, he would never see that woman again. *If necessary, I'll say goodbye to the fucking Oracle too*, he thought. He walked to the gym, intending to run on the treadmill as fast as he could, to

44

exhaustion.

"Sir," came Renith's voice from behind him. Zig spun around and began choking him against a wall.

"What!" he shouted. Then he let go, embarrassed. There were a few onlookers shaking their heads. "Sorry, I'm having a really bad day."

"If you want to change rooms, you have to pack and go to the receptionist right now, sir." Renith touched his hand to his throat, then smiled. "Damn, I never realized how dangerous you could be! I'd love to take out our frustrations at the gym. How about after we've unpacked?"

"Sure, thanks!" Zig made a tiny attempt at a smile.

While he was unpacking in the penthouse his phone rang. "Good afternoon, may I speak with Mr. Sanescid, please?"

"Yes, this is he, who's talking?"

"I'm Herman Steiner, director of the Pinakothek. I wanted to apologize on behalf of the staff."

Zig wondered why. He waited.

"I understand that Mr. Brenne was rude to you?"

"We had a hard time understanding each other," said Zig, who had a tendency to blame himself after a lifetime being blamed for everything.

"I was looking forward to meeting you at the award cele-bration, but you, Mr. Xenium, Miss Wills and many others weren't there."

"I wasn't invited, sir. I don't know about the rest." Zig's voice sounded dry as he said it and he felt a pang on his chest.

"That's what Mr. Xenium's representative told me, and I'm very sorry for the misunderstanding, Mr. Sanescid."

"There was no misunderstanding, sir, I was never invited, but I accept your apology." He wanted to finish this conversation.

"Goodbye."

"Please, let's not end like this! I want to invite you back, to present your excellent work. We'll pay you twice the amount..."

"No, thank you, Mr. Steiner. I'm not interested in staying longer. If you are interested, I can leave my paintings. To be honest, I really believe that my work doesn't need an interpreter. Otherwise, I'm a failure. Are you interested in that deal, sir?"

"Absolutely! Until when can we have your paintings?"

"Until the period you'll have the others, I guess. Goodbye, sir."

"No, wait, please!" said Steiner, hastily. "I know I have no right, but could you help us convince Mr. Xenium to participate, and explain him your wish yourself? Mr. Brenne's bad attitude has affected everyth..."

"I will talk to Mr. Xenium, and I wish you the best of luck, Mr. Steiner. I really need to go," said Zig, not only because he wanted to finish settling in to his new room, but also because he was too shy to have any conversation on the phone for more than a few seconds. This one had already been too long.

Once installed, he and Renith went to the gym and did their best to beat each other. It left Zig completely free of anger, but exhausted and bruised. "Thank you, Renith. I really needed this."

Renith was just as exhausted, and very impressed by Zig's abilities. How did he learn to fight when he'd been a slave? Unless he was being trained to fight... "How did you learn all those moves, Zig?"

"It's weird, but somebody has talked to me in my head all my life, since I left Sanescid. I called him my *lagun ikusezina,*

46

my invisible friend. Whenever I could, mostly when I was exhausted at night and sleep wouldn't come, we'd connect and chat. Night after night, he would teach me many things, among them how to fight and how to defend myself," he explained, "but I never had a chance to practice until I got here." Since he left Ethrea he hadn't heard that voice. He wondered why, and hoped that, whoever it was, they were okay. If the voice hadn't come from his imagination, or the Oracle, that is. "I need a shower."

In the shower he remembered that he had promised to call Nick.

Meanwhile, Renith wondered about that *lagun ikusezina* Zig was talking about. Was it his own imagination or someone real? They would definitely be Ewanian. He added that information to his e-notebook.

* * *

Damn, Zig thought, *I'm nervous.* Would Nick bother to answer? After only a year living in this world, so advanced compared to the one he'd come from, he still had a hard time using these magic devices and was very shy about them. He hadn't dressed yet because he wanted to be done with the call first. He knew that otherwise he was going to "forget".

He scribbled what he was going to say: *Hi. May I talk to Nick, please?* No, that didn't sound right, he scratched that. *Is this Nick? Hi! This is Zig. Oh, by the way, still very sorry about the beating, haha.* Shit! *Mr. Steiner, from the museum, called me to apologize and invite me to go back and leave my work for a little longer while getting paid. I made peace with him and am leaving my paintings. I think that you should too, unless you have some other reason you don't want to.* He held the paper in front of him and read it through again. He dialed.

"Hullo?"

Zig didn't recognize the voice. A bad start. "Uh... may I speak to Nick, please?" he said.

"Nick can't talk right now. Who's speaking?"

"Zig." He was horrified! Nick still couldn't talk, oh gods, that was bad!

"Ah, kiddo. What do you want?"

Zig guessed it was Mr. King, though he didn't dare ask. He was so embarrassed. "A message for Nick, please?"

"All ears."

Zig practically read what he had written. "*Mr. Steiner called me...*

"OK, bye." Click.

Ok, that was done, not as he had expected, but nothing was happening as expected that day. He was probably never going to see Nick again, and it hurt.

7

So They Were Real!

They had walked through the Gardens to the Platz. It was a beautiful sunny day. They decided to have lunch in one of the biergartens, but no beer this time, just juice. Aileen had already told Ulrich what had happened.

"I should have gone with you, Aileen. I'm sorry I didn't."

"It's done, love," she said. "It's all so bizarre, though. I dreamed about this young man in a strange land, a land I could never find during years of research, but there he is. It seems that he even recognized what I was describing, as if he had lived there. I can't be mad at him for what he said to me, especially if he did suffer as much as I recall in my dreams. Honestly, I have no idea what I was expecting. I should have prepared myself for something like this. I hope the kid's not as damaged as I fear he is."

After, they went to Saint Peter's Church and walked inside, absorbing its beauty, but they were also shocked to see skulls of bishops on the wall. They climbed up the turret, from which they could see all of the beautiful city of Munich. As they climbed back down to the church, Aileen had the urge to sit for a while on a bench. As a child, she had always heard from her grandmother that God was always there, that it was His home, and she believed it. She would still be a fervent Catholic if the church hadn't been so closed-minded about certain topics such as divorce and remarriage, especially when people in these situations many times made a better life for themselves, their children, and community. Then there were the problems they had with rights for gay people to marry, and birth control, among others. Aileen could understand, though, that the church would not approve abortion, because it is the termination of a life after all. Actually, that was always a tough topic. Ulrich, on the other hand, was an atheist and the only thing he enjoyed about religion was its music and art.

"I want to sit a little and meditate," she said.

Since Ulrich was also tired of walking, climbing up and down—"Those stairs were tough"—he agreed. They sat beside each other.

Aileen closed her eyes and prayed for clarity. She began to relax. As she let go, she allowed herself to imagine that her old dreams could be, in fact, real. It was clear that Zig was, and a lot of her dream must be too. Proof of this was his reaction towards her, especially to the word 'M'Anier'. He had been that very unhappy child, abused by everyone, so his reaction to anything dealing with that period was probably unbearable. If all of them were real, that whole family had been very unhappy, though they should have had everything to the contrary! They were, apparently, a weak and insecure king, an exiled wife, condemned to live imprisoned in the servants' quarters, a very lonely daughter… She wondered what became of Ariadné, the beautiful, sweet girl, and of Zig's twin brother, Sendoa, who would inherit everything and was educated to be the next king.

She remembered how the brother seemed so unhappy as well, the only time she had seen him in her last dream. She prayed for all of them, even for the king, *Please, give him a little bit of wisdom!* She opened her eyes and saw Ulrich walking back and forth, like a lion pacing its cage. "Time to go," she said out loud. They walked back to the hotel and went up to their room to pack.

8

"Good Bye Lagun Ikusezina

It was very dark, but he could see somebody shackled to the wall. They seemed to be unconscious, breathing with difficulty. It was a man, his long dark hair matted, probably with blood. He couldn't see the details, but the man had been badly beaten, that was clear. Zig was floating around, trying to make sense of what he was seeing. At first, he thought he was seeing himself, what had happened a year ago, when he had been so badly beaten that he was out of his body, looking at that foreign corpse that was his own. However, this one wasn't him. There was no mark by the right eye on this man, who looked unmistakably like him. He remembered seeing himself swollen, just like that. He looked up and saw a light attached by a golden rope to that broken body. Then he heard a voice call him 'friend.' "Nire lagun! You are here! Now I know what you must have passed through! It's so sad that we'll never meet, but I'm so happy that you are safe now." It was his lagun ikusezina, the invisible friend whom he'd always spoken with in his mind, since he was sent away, when he was just a child. He didn't even know how old he had been. "No!" He wanted to hold him, to take him away from that place. He wished it was

52

only a nightmare!

"Don't let the lady go," another voice said. *"Don't kill the messenger."*

He sat up with his eyes wide open, gasping for air. "My brother, oh God... He's dying. They are killing him! I have to follow... Don't kill the messenger." He got up and ran to the door. Renith was already waiting to stop him.

"Calm down. What's going on?"

"I need to talk to the lady."

"It's five o'clock, sir. You had a nightmare. You are safe here, calm down." Renith was trying to be soothing, a job that had belonged to Jeannie. He sounded rather grumpy instead. He'd been woken up suddenly, so he'd jumped to grab his gun and run to Zig's bedroom. "It was a nightmare, everything is ok now."

"It wasn't a nightmare! Worse! It was the Oracle! I messed up bad! My brother... They are torturing him, and I don't even know where he is! Oh Gods!" Zig said desperately. "I need to reach the lady I met yesterday, dammit, I insulted her! She'll not want to see me now!"

"At least dress up. Just wait for a more decent hour."

Zig grabbed whatever he had to hand and ran into the corridor, though in truth he had no idea which room was Mrs. Blight's. He just let his instincts take him, and wound up, to his surprise, right opposite the door to his old room.

Renith hung back, giving him space.

* * *

There was a knock on the door. Aileen was in the bathroom, wondering who'd knock so early. She heard Ulrich answer and heard him say, "No. She's not available. No. We're leaving..."

"Who is it?" she said.

"The young man, Zigor?" Ulrich replied.

"Tell him to wait for me in the restaurant. I need to drink a cup of coffee before we leave, anyway," she said.

"You heard her," he said, and closed the door. "But, Aileen, he was very rude with you!"

"Love, remember our conversation yesterday? I want to help that poor kid, if I can. I don't think I can do much, but for some reason I had dreams that affect him. I'm sure that he didn't mean to hurt me."

"But I'll be with you this time," he said.

* * *

Zig stood by the door, determined to stay there as long as he had to, because he feared he would lose her. For some strange reason, perhaps because of the dream, he connected her with his probably dying brother. As if his brother's fate depended on the talk they were going to have. It was very strange, but by then he was not going to question the Oracle.

He couldn't remember ever being together with his brother, except for a dream he had had since he was very young, about two or three years old. Both boys were playing happily, when suddenly someone, very violently, grabbed him by an arm and hit him in the face, hard. After that, all was dark. That dream repeated many times, reason he had created an antipathy, a phobia against the idea of ever meeting that brother. When older it had turned to hate, because he knew that Sendoa had everything while he had nothing. Also, because his brother never even tried to get closer. On the contrary. He distanced himself from Zig as far as he could, as if he had the plague. What he always had as company, though, was a voice that talked to him, and he could talk back. In the beginning, he would talk out loud, but then he got beaten for talking, so he tried to talk in his mind, and it worked just as well. From then on, he had his friend. Now, because of the dream, he thought he knew who really was his *lagun ikusezina*. Had it always been Sendoa? After wishing the worst things on his brother, whom he realized he didn't know at all, he feared that his wishes were coming true and now he was sick to his stomach. He wished that his dream wasn't happening. His *lagun ikusezina* hadn't talked to him since he had been rescued. Then he had thought it had been because of the distance between the planets. Now, he wasn't sure. His friend's voice in the dream had been clear and loud, coming from that light connected to his twin brother. A tear began to fall. *Maybe it's too late. If so, the Oracle has been laughing at me.*

Renith approached him. "Sir, let's go to the restaurant, it would be better."

"No." He was openly crying, but trying to compose himself. "If I miss her this time, I'm sure my brother will die." Zig's voice was coarse and a little louder than he wanted.

"You don't have a brother!" said Renith. "You were implanted in a womb. Whoever was in that womb is not your brother."

"I don't care how you call it, he's my brother and he's about to get killed!" said Zig, his voice a little louder still.

On the other side of the door, Ulrich was getting upset about the noise outside. He wanted to head to the lobby but didn't dare leave Aileen there with those men. He finally opened the door. "Weren't you supposed to wait in the restaurant? And who are you anyway?"

"I'm sorry!" said both.

"Zigor?" said Aileen. "Please come in. Are you with someone else?"

"I was just... leaving, ma'am," said Renith.

"But, Aileen!" Ulrich was beginning to lose patience.

"Love," she said, "it'll be ok, right Zig?"

He nodded and said, "I'm sorry, sir." He looked at the floor, waiting for a blow he was not going to answer. He'd been used to receiving blows for so much less.

Ulrich looked at the big, strong man and imagined himself crushed by the kid's thumb, but his face was that of a contrite puppy after it had done mischief. He let him in and left the door ajar.

"Please sit down." Ulrich sat on an opposite armchair and observed Zig, as if he were a case study.

Zig was so embarrassed that he couldn't take his eyes off the floor. He felt uncomfortable sitting at the same height. All his old habits came back, so he crouched as much as he could to be, as he saw it, in his place.

"I'm almost ready," said Aileen, coming out with a comb in her hand.

Zig knelt on the floor, begging for forgiveness. "I was horrible to you, Mrs. Blight, and I'm very sorry!"

She couldn't stop herself. She touched his head and caressed it, feeling innumerable scars, probably old wounds. He was very tense, but allowed her to continue. She bent down to face him. "Zigor, there's nothing to apologize for. I know you've been through a lot," she said. "How can I help you?"

He cleaned his tears with his sleeve, then looked at her. "Please, tell me everything about your dreams. I... I promise to not interrupt you."

"In that case, please sit comfortably while I ask for breakfast."
She went to get a tissue to give him and then faced Ulrich, who
had been watching them, less worried now.

"I'll go to the lobby," he said. "You, young man, will take care
of my wife. Promise?"

Zig, already seated with the tissue in his hand, couldn't
believe how understanding this couple were being with him,
and felt even worse. "I promise, sir," he said.

"What would you like for breakfast?" Aileen almost said
"son," but then realized it probably wasn't a good idea.

"I'm not really hungry, thank you," he replied.

"I'll ask for plenty. Then you take whatever you want, ok?"

"Sure, thanks."

She called reception and ordered. Then she began to tell
him everything from the very first dream, as best as she could
remember. She had a journal about these, but it was at home,
so she promised to send him a copy the minute they were back.

* * *

Could there be a brother? Renith was just a soldier. He
didn't have enough information to take any decision. Zig's
desperation made him very uncomfortable. Those were the
times he was supposed to call his superior.

"What's up?" said a voice.

"Sir, Zig's talking about a brother," said Renith.

"And?" It was obvious that he must have had a 'twin.'
Otherwise, how was he to survive from zygote form if not
by sucking from the woman's natural child?

"He's awfully worried about his whereabouts. He thinks his
brother's in danger."

57

"You might have to tell him that his brother is already dead. We wiped all the Sanescidians we could, after all."

"He woke up after a nightmare, dead worried about his brother."

There was a pause. "We wiped them all. There's no brother. Tell him that, it's an order."

"Yes, sir."

* * *

Zig wasn't only listening, but was also reading her mind, to check anything that could help him better visualize the images she was recreating while telling the story. It wasn't really necessary, though, since he was discovering that Aileen was very good at details.

"Wait! The woman had a mark on the side, like mine?" He was confused. Hadn't he been abducted by someone else? Weren't they blaming the Xanaduans? Maybe it had been a faction of renegades. Why hadn't they told him instead of... Damn it! How could he trust anybody? Except for the Oracle.

"Yes," she said, "They called them Oksaleb. They hated and feared them at the same time."

So, the same Oksaleb had done this! "Sorry for the interruption. Please go on."

She continued, with almost no interruption. At some moments, he would move nervously, look at her intently, or fidget with his hands. When she described to him how she wanted to say goodbye to her children before dying, how her soul flew to the market to find Ariadné chasing after him, he choked. He vaguely remembered someone chasing him and calling his name, but he'd run as fast as he could, fearing that he was in trouble, again. He had still been in pain from an earlier beating. He hadn't wanted another so soon.

"You ok, Zig?" Aileen asked, worried.

"I had no idea that she was my sister! I ran because I thought I was in trouble."

Of course not! How could he? He'd left so young, and when his sister saw him, she was already a young woman. Aileen held his hand and caressed it slightly. She feared that he would pull back, but he didn't. Finally, he was beginning to trust her. That felt good. She continued her description till the end. There was a minute of silence.

"You never had a chance to see my brother, except when you were dying, then. Could you tell me again that part? Please tell me with as many details as you can."

"When my spirit went to where Sendoa was, on the way, I heard a commotion. Many people were gathering on the main road, praising someone that was leaning out from a very fancy, but sturdy carriage with white handkerchiefs, which meant victory. The doors of the *gaztellu* opened and the carriage rolled in, with some of the soldiers surrounding the carriage, but most spreading around town greeting and hugging friends and family." She was puzzled because she hadn't remembered this dream with so much detail even when she'd dreamed it! She hoped she was not letting her imagination fill in the blanks. "The carriage got into the castle grounds and nobody seemed to be waiting for him inside. He stepped out and thanked the rest of the soldiers, saying, 'It's time for you to go to your loved ones. Thank you for the incredible bravery you all showed. I'll see you for training next week.'

"'Hail to the Prince, Hail to Sanescid!' they shouted together, before scattering slowly. He arrived at the fencing grounds, very proud, but bitter. Nobody was waiting for him..." Her voice was trembling, and her eyes burning. Tears began to fall, which she couldn't control.

Zig held her hands this time. "You were there, *Amak*," he said. She knew that meant 'Mother.'

"Can I hug you?" she asked, and they hugged hard and for a long time. She smelled him and really felt as if he were her own son. He wasn't, but she would adopt him, as well as his sister and twin brother if she ever could.

He heard her thoughts loud and clear. It made him feel much better. He could barely imagine finally having a mother, but he already knew he could trust her.

"So," she said finally, "can you explain to me what Ethrea and Oksaleb mean? And where is Sanescid? I've done research but nothing comes up. Because the dreams were so vivid, I'd been trying to find you and your siblings, but I could never get anywhere."

Zig took a deep breath. "Oksalebs come from Ewan," he said. "It's a very advanced world, from where people can travel all around the universe, including through time. Ethrea is another planet that has humans similar to the ones here, a little different to Ewan. Its people live in what I guess to be the equivalent of the Graeco-Roman period of this planet. Many places still use slaves, as you saw in your dreams of Sanescid."

"So, what do you call us?"

"Etwo. This planet is halfway advanced." He didn't say more about the topic.

Aileen was still pondering how it was that she'd started to have the dreams.

"I had a horrible dream last night," Zig said suddenly. "I saw my brother dying, and I don't know what to do! How can I find him to save him?" His voice broke.

"Can your people help you? Your friend outside seems a good person, he seems to care for you, what's his name?"

"You don't understand. Before you told me about the dream, I was told that the Xanaduans had abducted me, to destroy my people. But your dreams reveal something completely different."

She wondered what Xanaduan meant, but it was a question for another time.

"They lied to me. How can I trust Renith? Maybe he belongs to the same people that abducted me? If the woman in the birth room was Oksaleb, the same Oksalebs probably did it! How can I know? Who can I trust?" he said.

"Perhaps Renith was told what he's told you," she said. "Maybe he doesn't know either."

"Perhaps," he said. *After all, he's just a soldier. He doesn't receive much information, but he obeys orders without questioning,* he thought.

"Can you be sure to trust him?" Aileen wondered.

"I'll read his mind next time."

"What's that?"

"I can read minds, *Amak.*"

Shocked, she wondered if he had done that to her. She felt it was rather too intrusive, and looked to him for an answer.

"I don't do it unless necessary, I promise," he said.

"And you did it just now!" she said.

"I didn't need to," he said, telling a white lie. "Your description and expression said it all. I swear, I'll never do it unless you give me permission."

"Ok, son," she said. "I understand, but promise me that you'll let me know first, at least."

"I promise." He'd feared that he would lose her again, and it felt so good to have a mother, even if it wasn't real.

Then he remembered. "I think I can trust someone I know who's very powerful, but is probably very angry with me."

"Who's that?" asked Aileen.

"Someone I met before yesterday, but we did not part on good circumstances." Mr. King. First, he is also from Ewan, second, Renith had respected him, and third, Nick had mentioned that he was powerful.

"Can you reach him now?"

"Yes, but he might not want to help."

"Give it a try," she said. "Worst case scenario…"

He dialed the number. "Hello?"

"Jesus Christ! How stalker can you be? At this time of the day! Nick's still unavailable, kid," said King.

"I, sorry, please don't hang up! I want to speak to you, sir," said Zig. "I need your help!" He expected King to ask why he should do anything for him and was crossing his fingers that he wouldn't hang up.

"Explain," said King.

"I fear my brother is about to get killed," said Zig.

"You have a brother? An identical twin brother?" said King.

"Yes." Zig couldn't understand why everyone asked him that in such disbelief. When he got rescued, he hadn't bothered to mention his brother, first because he hated him and had blamed him for all his misfortunes, but also because he hadn't seen him for so many years and he was sure nothing bad was going to happen to him. He was convinced that the massacre that had happened had been to the ones that had beaten him almost to death. At least that was the threat that the Oksaleb woman had given. Why would they go to Sanescid, for what purpose when he was so far away? Now he feared that they had, *You do not want to hurt that child. If you kill him, the Oksalebs will destroy all you hold dear*, was what Mrs. Blight had dreamed.

"Can I read your mind, Zig?" said King, his voice softer, clearly more concerned.

Even though Zig feared King, he trusted him too. "Yes, sir." He opened up completely.

"Oh, yes, I agree. The kidnappers were Oksaleb. Now, concentrate on your dream. Tell me in detail all about it." Zig did. When he was able to visualize his brother, just like in the dream, King said, "Ok. Now you'll do something that's a little harder: lift yourself up as if in an elevator until you can visualize the place from above."

That was something that Zig hadn't ever done. On the other hand, he had dreamed it, so he was sure it could work. His brother's wellbeing was too important to him, so he let go his doubts and did his best. In his visualization, he lifted himself up. He then could see the building where his brother was. It seemed to be a small tower, very similar to so many in the south and center of Ethrea. As he kept on rising, he saw the building was in a valley surrounded by mountains, bigger to the west than the east. There was an old forest, too, which had been cut to the east, probably for farming. He had no idea where the place was.

"Thank you, Zig. You did a great job. I know where your brother is," said King. "Now, let's hope we find him alive."

"Sir, can I go with you?"

"I'm not going. As you were telling me I was sending the information to Ewan rescuers. I'll let you know how things come out. Meet me at the Pinakothek at one for lunch. If I know anything earlier, I'll let you know, ok?"

"Yes, sir," said Zig, "Thank you for everything. Please say hi to Nick."

"Will do, bye for now." He sounded grumpy, but he hadn't hung up. Zig thought maybe he'd forgiven him, or would eventually.

"How did it go?" said Aileen. They were supposed to be leaving that very minute, but she felt compelled to stay with him a little longer, now that he might receive very bad news.

"Better than I thought," he smiled at her. "They found the place where he could be. I only hope they rescue him alive." Tears began to run again on his cheeks, and he covered his face with his hands.

She went to get him another tissue, and was going to comfort him, like a mother would, when the door opened. It was Ulrich.

Time to go, she knew, but now she felt the need to be by Zig, who was quietly sobbing. She passed him the tissue and gave him a kiss on his head.

"We'll miss the shuttle, love," said Ulrich.

"Thanks, Mrs. Blight," said Zig, "I'll be ok. I have a few people that could stay with me if I need it. If they find my brother, I'm going wherever he is. I don't think I'll be here long."

"You got my phone number?"

"Yes, *Amak*. You got mine?

She didn't. "Call me whenever you can. Then I can save it on mine."

"Can I help you with the bags?" he said.

"No, sweetie. It's only one. Ulrich and I like to travel light." They hugged. Then, she passed him her room card. "Here, in case you want solace."

"Thank you!" he said.

Ulrich stretched out his hand and they shook. "Take care,

son."

"Thank you. Sir. I will." He wanted to call Ulrich *Aitak*, but felt more embarrassed about it. Also, that word brought him horrible memories.

They left.

He would stay in the Blights' room for a little while. He felt exhausted, so much that he fell asleep.

9

The Waiting

"Hello John."

"Bad news?"

"Guess so: some bad, some maybe good. Which one do you want to know first?"

"I'm an optimistic guy, bro. Give me the bad one first."

"Seems that someone from your district kidnapped your grandson, apparently when a zygote. It was never a Xanaduan, and before you ask any more wasteful questions, read my mind."

"Oh, shit!" said John. "That can't be! By my own daughter, their mother? Why?"

"But that's not your daughter, is she?"

"No, but she's her best friend..., unless their friendship fell apart and turned to enemies? The good news?"

"Hopefully good: Zig has a twin brother."

"And? All zygotes need a twin."

"An identical twin brother."

"Oh!"

"But he might be dead. Seems that your people intended to kill all the Sanescidians."

"What are you talking about? Oh gods! Where have I been to not know this? This is horrible! Do you know where he is, the brother?"

"Zig communicated with him last night and found where he was through a dream. He managed to give us the coordinates, but the kid was dying. Rescuers are there as we speak."

"Thank you, Dave. Please keep me informed. You've been always the best one. You should have been the king, man."

"Have never wanted the job and don't want it now. I trust that a governor chosen by the majority should have it."

"And what about the Oracle?"

"Fuck the Oracle. You know we lost, bro."

"I thought we hadn't in Oksaleb. Now it seems that I fucked up too. Please take care of Zig, and his brother, if he's still alive. What's his name?"

"Sendoa."

"The strong one. Let's hope he is as strong as his name."

"I'll send you news as they come."

"Thank you. One more time, you are the best. I'll raise hell here; it's shameful that I don't know what the heck is happening in my own country! Tell... no, better give Renith one of your phones. I'll give him my orders from here."

"Will do. Bye, brother."

"Bye, Dave. Thanks again."

"Hullo?" It was the first time this phone had rung. Zig was edgy.

"Hey, Zig. David talking."

"David?"

"King."

He should have known. Who else had his phone number, but Mr. King and Nick? "Sorry, sir, I guess I forgot that your name was David." *I'm so paranoid!*

King did not miss this thought. "Be paranoid, son. You need to be. That's why I was calling you. You can trust in Renith, though, as I told you before. He will follow instructions from us because he's a good soldier. I want you to bring him for lunch too."

"Yes, sir." But King had already hung up. How annoying! And he had read his mind without permission. On the other hand, why shouldn't he be rude? Zig had done something horrible to Nick. He knew that Mr. King would never forgive him. He wasn't forgiving himself!

He was still in the Blights' room and wanted to stay there a little longer, to lie down and close his eyes, try to relax.

* * *

Zig and Renith were sitting at one of the tables at the café when David arrived with Nick.

"Hey, Zig, so good to see you!" said Nick.

Zig still felt very embarrassed, "Sorry for what I did to you, Nick. I'll never forgive myself."

"Don't say that," said Nick.

"Why didn't you defend yourself, by the way?"

"Xanaduans have done so many awful things, including killing David's identical twin, Rick…"

"That's not true," said David.

"Yes, it is," said Nick. "My brother did it…"

"Because mine asked him to!" said David. "He was suicidal! I can't blame your brother, Nick! You have to realize once and for all that your sacrifice is bullshit! Next time, you defend yourself. It's an order."

"Fight a kid?"

"Who's trying to kill you? Yeah!"

"It won't ever happen again, Mr. King," said Zig.

"Doctor," corrected Nick with a grin.

"Why don't we order?" said David. The waiter had been hovering for a while, observing the strange discussion.

Once they had ordered and the waiter had gone, Zig idly wondered why doctors couldn't be called mister, like anybody else. *On the other hand, they save lives, I guess they have a right to be called whatever they want.* Zig had been waiting to ask King if he knew anything about his brother, but he still felt terribly embarrassed.

David noticed. "We found the place where your brother should be, but we haven't been able to find him."

"Oh, no!" said Zig. "He might be dead by now!"

"Let's hope not," said David, "but you must be prepared for any possible outcome, kid. Have you felt or heard his voice?"

"No," said Zig, fearing to ask if that was good or bad.

"That's good. Let's hope he doesn't come to you to say goodbye yet."

Zig nodded. For some reason, he didn't care any more that this man read his mind. He felt him to be like family, though he couldn't figure why.

"Ok," said David, looking at Zig. "We are here to find out why you and your brother were abducted by our own people, but first I want to introduce myself. I am Dr. David King, younger brother of Dr. John King, your grandfather."

Zig opened his mouth. A real family? They had already explained to him that he was no relation to the crown of Sanescid, but this man in front of him was telling him that he was family! He wasn't sure what that meant, though. Actually, he had no idea what a family was, it was just words to him. But, for real? His mind was spinning.

"That makes me your great-uncle," continued David.

Zig had turned a little red.

"And I hope that you trust me. Though, after all the mess you've lived through, you probably don't trust even yourself."

Zig thought of Mrs. Blight.

Except for Mrs. Blight, of course, David wanted to say, but he didn't want to irritate Zig any more. He had to tell the kid to shut himself down a little, but it would have to be another time. "Renith," he said instead, and took a phone from his pocket. "Take this. You'll receive orders directly from my brother, John."

Renith was shocked, though excited. He'd never imagined he'd work directly from one, much less two of the most important personalities of Ewan. "May I ask why, sir?"

"We fear that General Dwight might be part of the group that participated in Zig's abduction in the first place," said David.

"But he'll expect me to call him…"

"You'll continue giving him information like always from the phone he gave you and, once in a while, we'll tell you what to tell him," said David, "but you'll follow my brother's or my orders from this one—" He passed him the phone. "Try not to mix them up."

"Yes, sir, I can do this," said Renith, grateful that they were counting on him. Zig was growing on him and he'd felt the coldness of his former superiors towards the kid, as if Zig's welfare wasn't important, as if he was a pawn, something to be used for a higher scheme. Only now he had realized how important he was.

Meanwhile, Zig was looking at Nick, wanting to ask how he was doing. There was a small bruise under his right eye.

"So, Zig, I heard that you decided not to come to work at the museum. I have the feeling that it was the smartest thing," said Nick.

"It depends," said Zig. "Why did you accept? Did my call help?"

"I'm doing a personal study on the patrons, or visitors, actually."

"Really? What are you looking for?"

"Their reactions to my work. I'm recording the questions they ask and sometimes ask them specific questions myself. That's the only reason I am doing this. And, by the way, I'm also recording people that are asking about your work," said Nick.

"Why would you do that, man?" Zig was feeling embarrassed, again. "I did that stuff following the Oracle, and I came here following the Oracle, too. I don't even think that what I do is art. It makes me very uncomfortable to know what people think."

"You shouldn't. It doesn't matter why you do what you do. If people perceive it as art, then it is!"

"Look, the prodigal son!" cried Vivienne, who was approaching them. "How is it that you are here? I'd never step in this place again if they'd treated me like they dit to you. I almost rezigned! If not for him!" She pointed to Nick. Then she gave a big hug to Zig, who didn't know what to do, except reciprocate. "It's so goot to see you, Zig! How are you?"

"Er, ok, except worried for my brother. Nobody knows where he is." He wasn't sure what to tell Vivienne. He liked her a lot, therefore, didn't want to not tell her anything. He looked at David.

"Hi! I'm David King, Zig's uncle." David had his hand

extended to shake. Vivienne took it and saluted politely. David explained a more credible version of Sendoa's situation, that he had been kidnapped and they were asking for a ransom in some forsaken place in Africa.

"Oh, I'm so sorry!" said Vivienne.

There was an awkward silence.

Vivienne clearly felt uncomfortable, and was about to excuse herself when both Zig and Nick stood up to invite her for a walk.

David, now alone with Renith, said, "I want you to pay detailed attention to what the general tells you. Don't let him notice. Do everything as you've always done. Is that possible?"

"Yes, sir, though he might try to read me over the phone," Renith said. "But I'm good at hiding." He hoped he sounded confident.

David looked across at where Nick, Zig, and Vivienne were. "Nice girl," he said. "I hope she gets interested in Zig."

Renith said nothing, remembering Zig's relationship with Jeannie, which had been bad, very immature. But David was right. Vivienne was somewhat different, except that he couldn't imagine her interested in Zig, other than as a fellow artist. To start with, she was probably at least ten years older, if not more. On the other hand, it was already an asset just having her as a friend. To his surprise, he also felt that about Nick now.

"Good," said David, "let's eat," and he munched on a very appetizing hamburger with fries. Renith tucked into his lentil soup and a salad, looking disapprovingly at the food the doctor was eating. *Very bad for his health!* Perhaps Dr. David had been too long on this crazy planet, that he was acting like one of them.

Nick and Zig had sat on another table while Vivienne went to get her order.

"You sure Mr. King won't get mad that we left the table?"

"Dr. King," said Nick, "and no. He actually likes Vivienne, that's the reason he told her anything at all. She's a great person."

"How much does she know about you?"

"Nothing," said Nick, smiling. "I tell her what's believable."

Zig agreed. She already knew that he was worried about his brother's welfare. He'd tell her about his abduction and how his family was searching for him, though. Just thinking of his brother made him extremely anxious.

"I thought I'd never zee you again!" Vivienne was back from the counter, where she'd asked for a salad and a coffee. "So, you have a brother? Older or younger? You zeemed an only child," she said.

"Identical twin," said Zig. "My family is trying to find him, but I fear that it might be too late." His eyes filled.

"I'm zo zorry!" she said and hugged him. Then she looked at Nick, making a face. "Why are you involved?"

"I'm David's… partner." He turned red, embarrassed, wondering how Vivienne would take it that he was gay.

"How unlucky am I!" she said. "All the good ones are taken!"

Nick laughed. Then he turned serious. "David is in contact with the police and people he trusts and is receiving news as we speak," he said. "Since I'm working here, we thought it was a good place to meet."

"How can I help?" asked Vivienne.

"Just being here is great." Nick looked at Zig, who nodded. "Yeah."

10

What John Didn't Know

Equivalent to Tuesday, November 11 on Epsion, Oksaleb, Ewan. 5.30am.

"*General Dwight?*"

"*Governor. How may I help you?*"

I have heard from other sources that there was a holocaust in Sanescid, near a year ago. Do you know anything about it?"

"*I don't know what you're talking about, Governor. If so, it wasn't us.*"

"*Hmm. I understand that Zigor was in Tebas, where I also had heard of a massive reduction in the population, just after he'd been rescued. Anything you want to tell me, General?*"

"*No, sir. We didn't do such a thing. I swear.*" Too late, General Dwight noticed that his mind had been read, a sacrilege in normal circumstances, but not when suspected of serious wrongdoing. Suddenly he was surrounded by armed guards. Where had these men come from? How hadn't he noticed?

"*General. You are accused of at least two massacres. I have three teams working on finding out what else you were up to.*"

"*I was only following orders, sir! I thought they were from you!*"

WHAT JOHN DIDN'T KNOW

How dumb could he be! "Your daughter Marina gave the orders."
That wasn't true either, but nearer to it.

Marina... "So, you know where my daughter is, General?"

"No, sir. I just follow orders from her right hand, Ms. Alesandese.
The Sanescidians had treated Zig horribly. They deserved it, sir.
She ordered the deaths as punishment, Governor."

"Why on earth was Zig sent there in the first place, General?" If
the Sanescideans deserved death, what did his own daughter
and her best friend deserve?

*"I don't know, sir. I only followed orders." Yes and no. He had
gained something. What was not clear for John yet, was exactly
what that was.*

"Where is Gullivan, General?"

"I swear I don't know, sir." It was true.

ZAP! One of the guards shot him straight to jail.

Why on earth did they hide a zygote in Ethrea in the first
place? Whose brilliant idea was that? John kept on asking
himself, but it just didn't make sense. Nobody knew they had
this child, so their plan was to hide him. The zygote, as many
do, divided into two individuals: identical twins.

After observing Rick forever broken, and poor David, still
picking up the pieces, it was outrageous that his own daughter
had done it to her children. Rick had been abducted just after
they had been born by the Xanaduans, their eternal enemies.
Zig and his twin by his own mother? Why?

75

11

Sendoa is Found

He was looking to the star-filled sky. It was beautiful. He wondered then, why was he feeling so much pain? He realized he was on a cart, being pulled by a horse. The smell was unbearable. Why didn't he die once and for all? It didn't make sense. *Hey, friend,* he thought, *back to visit me, again?*

Hi, brother, thought Zig, *where are you?*

I don't know. It's been a long time that I have had no idea where they have me, or what they do to me. See? I try to sleep while they torture me. I think a lot of you. All your life, how could you stand it?

Seems they are being much worse with you than they were ever with me.

Zig started to rise up to try to see where they were, but Sendoa pleaded, *I feel so lonely. Please don't leave me! Stay with me till I die, please!*

You can't die, brother. We need to be together, don't die! He floated up to see where they were. It was so dark, he could barely see the silhouette of a horse carrying a cart, probably full of corpses. Among them was his brother, still alive. All was unbearably dark.

"NOOOO!" He woke up, sobbing. He sat up. It was still very dark. "Why can't they find my brother! Gods, help him!"

Renith was already by him trying to calm him down. It was useless.

Zig got up and phoned David. He didn't care what time it was, nor did he care about the yelling he was going to get.

"Zigor," said David. He didn't sound like he had been asleep.

"They are carrying him on a cart full of corpses! I couldn't see where to, it was so dark! He's dying, David, please help!" He couldn't believe that David could understand anything with all his sobbing. He was desperate.

"Close your eyes, kid. Try to get there again. I'll ask the team that's searching to make all the place as daylight. Please try to go back."

"Ok!" Zig closed his eyes and summoned his brother. There were the corpses tangled together. It was very dark still, but on his right side he could see a light that began to get nearer to where he was. He also noticed that the horse driver had detected it and was trying to go faster, scared of what it was. The light though, rapidly caught up to the cart and pointed over it.

A soothing voice then talked in the local dialect. "Stop the horse and we will let you go. Keep on and we will destroy both you and your horse."

The man calmed down the horse and made it stop. Then Zigor went back to his brother. His face was completely swollen and it seemed that he had lost one eye. His body was intertwined with other bodies. He looked up and saw smaller ships floating by in the air. David's men suddenly began appearing on top of the bodies. They began to work very carefully lifting corpse after corpse to untangle Sendoa. Nobody understood how he was still alive. It didn't make sense. Once they managed to free him, Zig saw that there was a silent airship above them, where the light emanated from. Something very powerful, but at the same time caring (if a machine ever could be) was lifting Sendoa up into the ship. He was limp. *Was it too late?*

"Now it's time to go, kid," said David over the phone, breaking the trance. "Grab clothes for at least a week and tell Renith to come too."

Zig was happy that Renith would be going, but for some strange reason he wanted Nick to come too. On the other hand, how dare he ever ask for that? He kept it to himself.

* * *

Zig and Renith were ready in the lobby as instructed. Nick came to meet them and take them to the car. That was a happy surprise. "So, you're coming with us?" said Zig.

"Of course, Zig. You are family to me," said Nick as they hugged.

"How about the exhibition?"

"Emergencies are a good excuse," said Nick.

They got in as fast as they could. Zig was too anxious to waste even seconds. The car looked very different this time. It had four seats and appeared similar to regular cars. But the moment they sat, something came out from both sides of the seat and wrapped around them. It was strange but comfortable at the same time.

The car moved smoothly out of the city into a desolate

road. Then, it lifted itself up into space as if there were no force of gravity. First, it lifted slowly, but then it accelerated exponentially until they were in black space. Zig could see the beautiful blue, white and brown round planet getting smaller as they distanced themselves. He felt exhilarated and scared at the same time. He couldn't remember how he had come to Earth in the first place. He had probably been unconscious still. He saw David push a few buttons while studying a three-dimensional space map that appeared in the air. Then, a green one.

Everything blurred as the ship moved. It felt as if it hadn't progressed at all, but was more like they were watching a video about traveling through space, except that Zig felt goosebumps in his skin. Very soon they were nearing a huge ship, where a pair of doors was opening on their approach. Inside it looked dark, like a mouth ready to eat them.

* * *

As David drove into the dark tunnel, dim lights turned on showing him where to land. They were received by a squadron of soldiers saluting him. Their commanding officer was besides someone resembling David King, but older, with lighter hair but darker skin. While David had hazel eyes, this man's were grey.

King got off, saluted back and walked to the man, whom Zig realized was David's brother. They hugged for a long time. Zig wondered if it was time for he and Nick to get out. He glanced at Nick, who seemed to be hiding behind the seat, trying to make himself invisible. "Oh, crap," he said. "You're scared!" Nick belonged to the enemy. Didn't David realize that? He looked back at David. He was still talking to his brother—Zig's grandfather!—who was looking into the car.

David and John approached. "This is Nick," David said loudly, inviting Nick out of the car. "He tried very hard to save my brother Rick's life, and did save mine. I wish you to treat him as a brother."

Nick was red, very embarrassed, and still nervous.

The assembled soldiers saluted Nick very respectfully and tried to hide their inquisitiveness, for most had never seen a Xanaduan.

"And this," David continued, inviting Zig out of the car, "is Zig King." Then to Zig, "I hope you don't mind that name. Sanescid doesn't deserve your name."

Zig smiled. "I like King, sir," he said. He did like it. Everyone applauded in welcome. Zig was moved, and blushed dark pink with the unusual sensation of people being happy he was there. Suddenly he was right in front of his grandfather.

"Come here, my grandson!" He hugged him, making Zig feel particularly awkward. Until then, only Mrs. Blight, Vivienne, and Nick had hugged him. Nobody else, ever before, except maybe awkward hugs from Jeannie.

Then Sendoa's image appeared in his head, "May I see my brother?"

His grandfather let go. "Sorry, yes. You should be there."

"And, let me introduce you to Renith," said David.

"Nice to meet you, Sir," said Renith, as he bowed in awe to meet another member of the famous King Ramos family. John bowed back with a smile.

"Let's go to the clinic," said John, inviting them all to come with him. He saluted the general and introduced him to David and Zig on the way. "This is General Michaels. Her squadron, with your help, Zig, finally found your brother."

"Thank you, General Michaels!" said Zig.

"It was an honor, Zig. What's his name?" said Michaels.

"Sendoa, ma'am."

"No wonder he survived. It's a miracle, you know?" said the general.

"He reminds me of Rick," said John, as they walked toward the clinic.

"Yeah, there is some similarity," said David, thinking of his twin brother.

"And you always behind, saving his butt."

David remembered. They had had a love/hate relationship. When they had found Rick, he already disliked him. During all his childhood he had been the invisible one because his brother's absence was a constant presence. Everybody was constantly looking for his brother, trying to trace the kidnappers, to no avail. Dave was permanently set aside or asked to be a good boy and thankful. That was what he was. By the age of eighteen he was among the best physicians of Ewan.

By that time Rick had been found in Ethrea. The first time that Dave laid eyes on his brother, he saw a strange being, identical to him, except for his wild stand towards life. It didn't matter the amount of years that would pass, Rick only managed to connect with Ewans in the most basic ways, and Dave played interpreter. He kept his recklessness and, wherever he was, he would fight for the weak, sometimes against very powerful people. David went behind, saving him from imminent death. Rick was a compelling young man who had his own followers. David felt the obligation to take care of his brother, even when Rick didn't want his help. Funnily, both had talked through their thoughts as *lagu ikuse zina* since toddlers, just like

81

Zigor and Sendoa, except that they didn't realize the sibling connection till many years later, when they had begun to care for each other. David had to admit they were similar, but it seemed that Zig and Sendoa had had it much worse. First, they were found in the most inhumane place of Ethrea, whereas Rick was found on the opposite side, among a tribe where he was some kind of a leader. And worst of all for the kids, someone from their own world, not an enemy, had done this horrible act on purpose.

When they reached the clinic, John introduced them to Doctor Zelop. She was a tall woman, probably in her thirties. She was still worried that Sendoa would not survive, partly from doctor's compassion and partly for her job security. It was the child of one of the most important personalities of Ewan, after all.

"Hello," she said, "I wish I could give you better news, but the patient is still between life and death."

"Please, ma'am... Doctor." Zig was trying to be as respectful as he could, still unsure on how to address the people he was meeting. "Can I see my brother?"

She took out her hand to shake it with Zig, and invited him in. "Doctor. You can call me Doctor, Zig, but it's ok if you call me anything you want. I'm Linda Zelop," she said. Then, looking to the others, "I don't think it's a good idea to come in all together, but his brother should be a good start." They all agreed and waited outside.

It was a large and dark room. Dr. Zelop gave Zig a pair of goggles. "With these you'll be able to see," she said. "For your brother must stay in the darkness, an environment similar to when you were in your mother's womb. Sorry, I forgot..."

"It's ok, Dr. Zelop, I understand," said Zig. When they had

rescued him, he'd been in one of these too, as he had been near death. He began to wonder how bad he had really been compared to his brother. *Sendoa surely is worse*, he thought. He put on the glasses and looked around the room. There it was, a round transparent container full of a very light yellowish liquid in a permanent, but slow flow. Inside was Sendoa, bent in a fetal position and floating in the liquid attached to something like an umbilical cord. His face had a mask, similar to the one Dr. King had put on Nick. His body was so bruised! Zig wondered if he'd been that bad, back then. He called his brother the way he used to do with his *lagun ikusezina*.

Hey, I'm here.

It's so good to see you brother. You look so healthy! Sendoa's thoughts came through clearly at least, despite his broken body.

Finally, I can see you. The doctor told me that you were still between life and death.

I was waiting for you. I'm very happy that you found your people. I lost it all. There's nothing for me now, but I did want to see you, to say goodbye. I'm ready to...

No, Sendoa, please, don't do that! You also belong to these people, don't you see? We are identical twins, we belong to the same family, the Ewans!

It doesn't make sense, Zigor... Sendoa started to move, as if to face Zig, but then he stopped. An alarm went off and Dr. Zelop came in to check what was going on. David came behind, very quietly.

"He wants to die." Zig was trembling, trying to contain his tears, talking to no one.

David hugged Zig and looked towards the chamber. *Nephew,* he thought to Sendoa, *you are like me.* He moved his head from side to side trying to show Sendoa that he had no mark. *You*

83

are my nephew, you are family. Please give yourself a chance to meet your brother and give him the same chance, to meet you. Then David faced Zig. "You gonna be ok?"

"I think so," said Zig, wanting David to stay with him while seeing how Sendoa deteriorated, but on the other hand, feeling that he had to do this alone.

Sendoa moved his head towards Zig, *They killed everyone! Women, children, they didn't care! They killed my girlfriend, the woman I was going to marry...* Sendoa shook his head.

Zig, full of tears, kept on looking at that battered body, convinced that it was going to be the last time he'd see his brother.

I'll do my best to live, I promise. Only for you. If you want me alive, it's the least I should do.

Zig began to breathe again. *Thank you, brother.* Then he touched the chamber with both hands and his cheek. Sendoa moved his body towards Zig and they both stayed there for a long time with their hands together, separated only by the clear chamber wall.

Dr. Zelop observed them and realized that Zig was not planning to leave his brother's side until Sendoa could get out of the n-womb or die. "You can stay here as long as you wish," she said. "We'll bring in everything you need."

"Thank you, Dr. Zelop."

"You're welcome, Zig," she said in a soft voice, and left.

* * *

David was looking at Sendoa's clinical history and, like everybody else, wondered how this young man had stayed alive. So that he could see Zig? To say goodbye? Make sure that he was ok? All his organs were almost shut down. Nothing was working inside that poor battered body. The n-womb was working at full speed to remake his organs and keep him alive. All the team was working overtime, not only because he was the grandson of John King, but also because they had never seen somebody with so much strength to fight the odds. Sendoa had, in no time, turned into an idol. He reminded them of Rick King, struggling for justice all around the universe, getting beat up to pulp, and practically resurrecting himself. Most forgot that he had been able to do this because he, David, was always behind, saving him. They were supposed to be the next generation of rulers, but everything went to hell.

Now David was alone, Rick gone, Ewan just managing. Were Zigor and Sendoa their next hope? Or was it too late? The only thing David knew was that he was not going to push it, nor let anybody do it either. The kids had the right to take the decision for themselves.

He sensed his brother's reckless spirit in Sendoa. *Why should I live when there's nothing for me here?* No connection or interest with Ewanians. Why should he have? Sendoa was living what Rick probably had when Ewanians found him thirty years ago.

What was different this time was that Zig was the one with the mark. He would be the ruler if they ever rule over Ewan. Sendoa would be his second-in-command. Both had to be alive and work together. That was why it never worked with Rick and him. They barely got to like each other until it was too late. Nor did they know that they were supposed to work together. David felt like Ricky's eternal servant. Too late did they realize that their *lagun ikuse zina* were each other. Back then, they could have done it, except that somebody destroyed that dream, the one who had killed Rick's wife and greatest

85

love. When they killed her, they killed him and nobody knew who her killer was. All they knew was that they had been Ewanian.

Dave took a last look at the twins. Sendoa was struggling against death. *I need to heal, bro*, he heard from his nephew, and then he disconnected himself into a coma. His body seemed more relaxed and his last move was to be near Zig, hopefully touch him by touching the n-womb wall. If he was able to heal, in a few days Sendoa would be out and meeting his brother for the first time in years.

Now we have to look for Sendoa's girlfriend, dead or alive, thought David. As he left, he saw Zig sitting with his back on the n-womb wall, against Sendoa's back. He finally seemed to be sleeping, while Zig had also his eyes closed, a slight smile on his lips.

12

Reminiscing in Paris

I t was windy and the leaves were spreading everywhere as it was autumn in Paris. The Blights were worried about stepping on dog poop. Aileen had forgotten how disgusting French dog-lovers seemed to be about their dog's business. Still, they were enjoying their walk, reminiscing about their time as university students. They had planned to visit all the touristic sites like the Eiffel Tower, the Palais Garnier, Les Invalides, Musée d'Orsay, Musée d'Orangerie (they both loved Impressionism), the Musée du Moyen Âge, the catacombs, and, of course, parts of the Louvre. But their main plan was to revisit the places they'd been when they were young, full of dreams, but penniless, around thirty years ago. Places like La Cité Internationale Universitaire, where they would go for lunch every day to save money, since their squalid room did not have a kitchen and it offered very good and cheap food, or they would stay away from the freezing winter inside the Centre Pompidou to read or study since the place they were staying didn't have any kind of heater. They remembered how excited they'd been when just arrived, watching all the French movies available, regular and avant-garde. Now, they were walking on Rue Riche where they had lived for a while on the top floor of an abandoned building. They walked the streets as they had had done then and ended up in front of the Moulin Rouge, though they were not interested in getting in. It was a landmark to revisit. Not much had changed. Then they took the Metro to Pigalle and walked toward the funicular to Sacré-Coeur. Aileen had lovely memories of this place. She remembered being invigorated inside this beautiful church as she learned that, during World War II, it had been destroyed by the Germans. Then the neighbors had worked together, collecting money from their humble salaries to rebuild it. She could feel all the love they had put into it.

Her phone vibrated. It was a text message: *Dear Amak, we found Sendoa, but it might be too late. He's dying! I'm lying by him. I hope to give you better news soon. Zig.* She wondered, *Where is he texting from? Any place on Earth, or in Space?* Though she found perfectly normal that he could text her from anywhere, she was moved that he had texted at all.

She stopped at the stairs and wrote back, *We are in the perfect place for praying for your brother. Our hearts go out to both of you, sweet Zigor. Love, Aileen.* She showed Zig's message to Ulrich. He embraced her, and she hugged him back.

Inside the church, she went straight to the benches and sat down to meditate, while Ulrich walked around. He realized that he liked Notre Dame more, with its crazy idea of building towards the heavens by just believing that it would stand by the grace of… what, a god? And it still stood!

They were going to visit Notre Dame the next day. Ulrich invited Aileen to light a candle, knowing that she would

88

appreciate it.

She knew there was no logic to doing any of these things, but it made her feel better. She went to the Virgin Mary's altar, thinking a talk from a physical woman to a spirit woman would bring her better results. She prayed for Sendoa. She thought that if he survived this ordeal, he and Zigor would finally have a chance to know each other. She was convinced that that would be a huge healing for both. If Sendoa died, it would be very hard for Zig to heal, so she prayed for both.

They left the church and walked without direction through the streets towards the bottom of the hill. Then, just outside of the touristic area, they had lunch at a café.

When they were back at the hotel, she received another text message from Zig: *He'll make it!*

Thanks! she thought. Then wrote him back: *I'm so happy for both! Love you, your Amak.*

The next day they went to the Centre Pompidou. Paris doesn't change much. That's its charm. Then, as promised, they visited Notre Dame. The next day they would dedicate to the Louvre.

Zig texted Aileen every day letting her know how Sendoa was doing, which was a miracle, after being so near to death. Zig's texts made her feel nearer to both brothers. She made a promise of treating these two almost strangers as her own children. In the dreams she had endured only a few years before, they were her own children after all. She kept her promise of praying for them both every day.

* * *

They almost accomplished everything they'd planned in Paris.

89

A day more in the Louvre would have been good, but you can only do so much. It was time to head back to Munich, and then back to Victoria. Both were missing home and wanting to go back to their routine.

Dear Zig, she texted. *We are heading back home, but I hope that you will keep us up to date about what's going in your life and your brother's. It's been a beautiful experience knowing you and I really hope you don't forget us. Please, wherever you are, know that you are in our hearts. If you come to the US or Canada, let us know. There's always a way we can see each other, not only to see you, but also to meet your brother. Love, Ulrich and Aileen (your Amak).*

The phone beeped back, *Dear Amak. Thank you. I promise to keep in contact and to visit if we are nearby. Sendoa is doing much better. He only needs to get stronger again. He still weighs so little and can barely walk. We learned that he had a girlfriend. We are searching for her now and hoping she's alive. I'll keep you posted, promise. Zig.*

13

Beatrix

After Sendoa had sent out a mental image of his bride, Beatrix of Heinne, they started the search. The area Sendoa had given them was empty. They could find clear tracks made by people and carts to the north, so they followed. After a hundred miles of desolation, there were signs of normality, nature untouched by the Oksaleb. There were farmed lands, but no visual signs of people. They were probably hiding, even though the airships roaming around were cloaked. John wondered if the people living there were hiding just in case the Oksaleb wrath repeated, this time against them. He was disgusted at the type of monsters his own people had turned into. He wondered since when and how was it that he'd been in the dark. How had he not known of this genocide? General Dwight must have been one of the perpetrators, but he had not been alone; he must have been following orders, but from whom? His own daughter? His son-in-law? What was in their minds? He was exhausted from asking himself the same questions over and over.

Luckily, they didn't need to disturb these fearful people.

They just scanned through looking for Beatrix.

"We think we found them, sir. There's a woman that matches the image Sendoa sent us."

"Thank you, General Michaels," said John. "Did they tell you if she's alright or hurt?"

"They said that she looked very well," said Michaels, "that she seemed to own the place where they were staying."

"Please, tell the soldiers to leave. All these people are scared to death of us. We'll handle it from the mothership." If it was Beatrix, she was safe. No need to act fast any more. Sendoa should take over this mission.

"But there's something else, Sir," said Michaels.

"Yes?" John didn't like the General's worried tone.

"Seems that Zig recognizes a lot of these people, and not in a good way."

"What do you mean?"

* * *

Zig had gone in one of the scout ships, with Renith, Nick, and a lead pilot. The ship was passing over a town. As Renith augmented the visual, checking for Beatrix and scanning the people around, Zig recognized many faces of those that had raped and tortured him, as well as other children like him. They looked older, but he was sure they were the same. They had rich dresses with Heinnean designs. That paralyzed him. He began to turn pale and bent down, gagging.

"What's going on, Zig?" said Nick.

Zig couldn't respond. It seemed that he was somewhere else, maybe reviving a traumatic experience from the past, thought Nick.

"Zig, it's us, your friends!" said Renith.

Nick was getting out of the seat, but the pilot told them to stay put. "We'll head back now. Stay tied on your seats, please."

The pilot tried to move back to the mothership as smoothly as possible but could not prevent Zig floating all over the place, hitting himself on the head and right side first, then the left and back of his head. Because he was bent as if protecting himself from whatever was happening in his mind, he did not hurt himself badly, ending up with a few bruises.

After they landed, Nick and Renith rushed to Zig's side, checking if he had hurt himself. They found him in a catatonic state. His eyes were wide open, as if reliving a horrible moment. Renith visualized what Zig was recreating in his memory. It was horrific. He hugged him, trying to get him out of it, but it was futile. Renith had no idea how to get him out. Nick watched, alarmed, also without a clue on how to help his friend.

"Zig?" said Nick.

Zig didn't answer. He wasn't even listening.

They asked the general for help.

* * *

When the search teams thought they'd found Beatrix, they sent an image to Sendoa. He recognized her, so he could finally relax. Why then was he having such a horrible stomach ache, to the point of wanting to throw up? He knew that that could happen if he had eaten but he hadn't. He'd been so emaciated when rescued that he still had cramps after eating and made huge effort to keeping the food down. This was different. It was agony, so deep! *Oh, Zigor!* He called mentally.

I can't be with you if you are with her, thought Zig back. *She...*

I... When Father sent me away... it was with them

Sendoa had another cramp. *Oh brother, I'm so sorry! Please breathe in and out, you are hurting, and it's hurting me too! I'm going to you now.*

I don't want to make you miserable, Sendoa, thought Zig. His stomach hurt even more and Sendoa almost fell, holding his abdomen with both hands.

David had been sitting beside Sendoa, so he noticed the change. As a trained doctor, he went through his thoughts to figure out what was happening, so when Sendoa asked him for help, he was already opening drawers, picking up a few medical tools and helping Sendoa up with his crutches. "Let's go," he said.

When they got to the landing hangar, Zig was still sitting inside the scout ship, accompanied by Renith and Nick.

"He doesn't seem to be here," said General Michaels. "He's reliving something that happened to him. Renith and Nick are with him, but he doesn't seem to recognize them." She was very worried. Only people with too much baggage had that level of PTSD.

"Thank you, General."

"*Kaixo nire lagun* – hi, my friend," said Sendoa. He knew Zigor was far away, in his hell. It was better to try his *lagun ikusezina* scheme.

"Hey!" said Zig. "I dreamed that I was in an amazing place, where people cared for me. It was so... How are you, *nire lagun ikusezina*? Seems I hadn't seen you for a while."

"I'm fine, I ..."

"In the dream I met my brother. He was you. Is it so?"

"Yes, it was always me, your brother. I hope you forgive me for not telling you?"

94

"I like it more. Are you ok?"

"Yes, bro."

While they were talking David opened a bottle that let a kind of mist float towards Zig.

"No," said Zig, "he was... my... best... friend. Are... you... *nire... anaia...?* My brother?" He slurred the last words.

"Yes. Can I hold you?" said Sendoa.

"Can... you?" Then Zig nodded and lost consciousness.

Sendoa held him while two men brought a floating stretcher. "What did you do to him?"

"Just to help him relax, so he can come back," said David. "I gave him a little extra dose because he was too far."

"Will he come back?" said Sendoa. He wondered if he also was going to have episodes of this kind. He had woken up screaming from horrible nightmares more than once. He wondered if it was the same.

"He will, and he may feel mortified. It would be a good idea that you stay with him to be there the moment he wakes up," said David. "You two have gone through similar experiences."

Sendoa shook his head, he was sure he'd lived nothing compared to his brother. His had been a mere and short purgatory compared to Zig's entire life in hell. He gladly went after his brother when they took him to his room.

What kind of horror had Zig suffered to end in that state? What had Beatrix and her people done to him? He couldn't connect the sweet and brave woman he'd been with just a few months ago with the woman he saw through Zig's mind.

They had been preparing for their wedding. They had secretly made vows to each other with a few of his soldier comrades as witnesses, part of the Heinnean wedding ceremony. Also, he had known Beatrix and played together with her since they were children. He knew that his brother had been brought to her house and had told her how much he wanted to see him, but that his father wouldn't let him. She'd promised that she would take care of him and he had trusted her.

"He'll be like one of my treasures," she had promised.

He knew she was too young to do anything, but he hoped that she would make a difference for his brother. How dumb had he been! Whenever Zig had been battered, Sendoa had thought it had been the adults, the servants, anyone, except Beatrix. He still hoped it was so. Zig's suffering was so huge that maybe he put everyone in the same basket. He was exhausted with the physical and emotional events of the day. He lay down beside his brother and felt the urge to sleep, wondering if David had sent some of the medicated dose his way too.

* * *

Zigor's PTSD was to be expected but David, John and General Michaels were worried that it could affect the job they had ahead. Michaels was concerned about the level of trauma. "If we follow the Oracle as we should, we would have to accept Zig as our leader," she said, "and right now he's not prepared. Nor is his brother," though she had better hopes for Sendoa.

"General," said David, "let's think about the immediate future, let's not get too far ahead. People pushed Rick to get to task, to be the leader and it was a total disaster. He wasn't ready, struggled alone against everyone, including me! We can't make the same mistake."

"David is right," said John. "Right now, I don't intend to let anyone make my grandchildren do anything they don't want to do. They need healing. Even better, let's allow whoever did this horrible deed to think that they won..." *And maybe they did*, he thought." We still don't know who did this, though we have clear suspects. If they think they won, we might have a better chance of discovering them." He hoped that they would let down their guard.

"Do they know about Sendoa?" wondered the General.

"I wonder myself," said John, thoughtful. "I still think it's a good idea to let them think that there's one kid, and that he's broken." Though he was hoping that the brothers enjoyed being themselves, without any burden of leadership, for a long time; that they healed. After, they would decide when to train the kids, only if they wished to.

David agreed. He realized that there were too many Ewans wanting to change the governing system. Since his brother's kidnapping as a baby, everything had changed. The Xanaduans had done it and they'd paid for it. Sadly, the Ewans never recovered either. Now things were not done by the Oracle, therefore everything was, according to some, a disaster, therefore these two young men were the hope for a way back to normalcy. David happened to disagree and was hoping for good old-fashioned democracy, which he thought was next to the best option. Let the kids be kids. If they healed and wanted to, really wanted to, they would govern. He did not share his thoughts.

14

"Don't Be Ashamed"

Both brothers woke up at the same time, though **Sendoa was the first to get up, which** he did very quietly, trying not to disturb his brother. When he turned to face Zig, he wanted to touch him, but pulled back, afraid of Zig's reaction. Zig probably wouldn't like it, he thought.

Zig opened his eyes, feeling his brother watching him, and they looked at each other, face to face. Confused, Zig was the first one to look away.

"Sorry! Just wondered if you were awake," Sendoa whispered.

"Yes, I think so," said Zig, turning back to Sendoa. "Unless this a dream?"

"No, bro, the other was the nightmare. How are you feeling?"

"Good, except for... horribly embarrassed," said Zig, remembering the visions he had and wondering how much of a mess he had made.

"Don't worry. All's good," said Sendoa. "We need to talk, though."

"Brother," said Zig, knowing what was next, "you have the right to marry whoever you want. I just don't think I can…" He hugged himself, as if wanting to disappear.

"That's what we need to talk about," said Sendoa shaking his head. "I don't think I want to marry her anymore if she hurt you like I saw in your mind, Zig. You are my brother. I want to get to know you, to be real brothers, do whatever brothers do. I just want her to be safe for the moment, that's all."

Zig still felt too guilty to understand what Sendoa was saying, but nodded. He thought that he would try to convince his brother to do what he really wished later.

"Hi there," interrupted David, who had just entered the room. "How are you feeling, Zig?"

"Better, sir. Sorry, I didn't mean to…"

"You did what you had to, kiddo. You did well, letting us know that there's something wrong out there. We will be better prepared now."

"I'd like to visit her," said Sendoa, and more to himself, "I'd like to see how she'll react seeing me." He was still very confused after seeing the images of Beatrix transmitted from the ship that had found her, looking so healthy and elegant. He had always thought that both of them had suffered the same fate. She seemed happy, not mourning his absence. "She got over my death too fast."

"Maybe she's practical and moved on?" said Zig. "But if she sees you again, she'll probably be very happy. I am."

"I'm very happy to finally be with you, Zig. It's the best thing that's happened to me since, forever!" But he wasn't sure about Beatrix. "That's why I need to go down and see her, but I'm so weak!" How could he show strength in the middle of lions when he was so damn fragile?

"You don't have to go in person," said David. "You can project yourself in the form you wish, let me show you both." He took them to the control tower of the mothership.

In the tower, John and General Michaels were scanning the three-dimensional images that the ships had taken and sent. It was a small city. It had beautiful old buildings decorated with murals of daily life activities. Then there were newer ones, built as if in a hurry. They had already studied the age of the buildings and type. The oldest ones were at least a century old. There had been more construction lately, which made them think that a larger number of people had immigrated.

"Good morning, boys," said John. "How are you feeling?"

"Good morning, Dr. John," said Zig, while Sendoa saluted the Sanescidian way, with a bow. Then he retracted, but John responded appropriately.

15

Sendoa's Projection

* * *

"**W**here were your girlfriend and her family living when you met her?" asked John.

"In Heinne. They were neighbors of our kingdom," said Sendoa.

"A hundred kilometers away," said Michaels, looking at a map on the screen. "Heinne."

"Yes, General," said Sendoa. "It was part of my father's domain, but they had their own government, like a principality."

"That's all gone," said Michaels.

"That's why I was so worried about her. They'd lost everything, but now they seem to be fine. So how does it work? I'd like to meet her," said Sendoa.

David showed him one of the projectors and explained to him how to use it. Sendoa went into a cylindrical structure.

"Imagine yourself the way you wish to be seen, now," said David. "You can also choose to touch and be touched, but that can be dangerous." If someone stabbed him in that condition, he could end up dead, even if he wasn't there. The power of suggestion was too strong.

"When you are projecting yourself, you can't read people's minds, either. Don't even try it because you might lose precious time for your survival."

"Ok," said Sendoa.

"Now, let's practice."

Sendoa got into the projector and created his avatar. He dressed himself in an elegant white garment he used to wear in the palace when hosting important visitors, with his sword to his side. Both things in reality were lost forever. "Ok," he said. "So, I can touch and be touched. Can I stab someone?" *If so, will it hurt or kill them?* he wondered.

"Yes, but I wouldn't try it. I know you are an amazing warrior, but you're going to be alone."

"I guess it wouldn't be clever. Don't worry, I won't try," said Sendoa.

David sent Sendoa's projection into the wilderness not far from the city, making sure nobody would be around. *Though it wouldn't be a bad thing if someone saw and told,* he thought.

Sendoa had decided to project himself with his senses included because he wanted to smell and feel the breeze. The place had overgrown grass with a few trees surrounding it. It felt a little cooler and greener than his native land, at least what it used to be. Now, he imagined a charcoal black and toxic wasteland. *Nothing would ever live there again*, he thought.

David read his mind and thought to tell him that they could fix it, but preferred to keep that to himself for now. There would be time to discuss that matter, and after all, they could only fix the landscape, not bring back the dead.

Sendoa stretched both arms down, feeling the dew on the grass, cool and wet. It was going to be a sunny morning, but the dew hadn't evaporated yet. "What time is it?" he asked David, not sure if he'd talked from the ship or his projection. That was weird.

"Around 6am," said David. "Anything you'd like to adjust?"

"Can I talk to you without looking foolish talking to myself?"

"You can use your thoughts and give me permission to read them," said David.

"Permission granted."

"Now, look at your right or left wrist. See a red button?"

"Yes."

"It's your emergency button. Press it if you feel in danger, or whenever you want to leave the place."

"OK." Sendoa thought that he wasn't going to need it. Beatrix had been more than a friend to him. Worst-case scenario, she would tell him that she wasn't interested in marrying him any more, and he was alright with that.

David was less trusting, "We need backup in case something goes really wrong. If you can't press the button, what sign will you give me, for help?"

"I saw this sign on a photo that Zig showed me yesterday." He made it with his left hand: 'l.'

David laughed, "Ok, I like it! Then we're ready?"

"Yeah."

Sendoa was walking with his hands touching the dew, feeling the softness of the long grass. Then he took his sword out and began to swing it around, cutting the tips. It felt so good, just the way it had when he was the most important soldier in the world, leading his men to battle, defending the vast territories his father reigned. He was so powerful, merely by being Kuiril's

103

son, though his men had learned to respect him for who he really was. A true warrior always caring for his men and his people. He stopped, looked down and knelt, closing his eyes. The wet grass touched his face, caressing him. He began to cry.

"What's happening?" said David, intuitively knowing something was wrong.

"They're all dead, my people." He pressed the red button and his projection began to fade.

"I'm so sorry, Sendoa," said David. "I promise we will find the culprits."

"I'd start with Kuiril, whom I thought was my father, if he's alive. He has a lot to answer," said Sendoa. "So, when do I go back?" His spirits lifted again, looking forward to seeing Beatrix.

"Depends on the time your princess gets up. We'll have to check what she's doing and find the best time. Meanwhile, you should have something to eat and relax."

I don't think she's my princess, Sendoa thought. Then, *Why is it still so hard to eat?* He couldn't understand it, his medical treatment was already over. He was still never hungry.

* * *

She was in the backyard of the palace, dressed in a soft silky dress, the style he had seen her wearing when he had visited a little over a year ago. The backyard had a huge, beautiful garden full of brightly colored irises on her left and red, white, and pink roses on her right. She was accompanied by a male friend who Sendoa remembered, and four guards were a little further behind, giving them privacy. She was radiant.

"Hello Beatrix," said Sendoa, walking over to them. "How

are you?"

She turned to him in shock, "What!? What are you doing here?" She seemed to shudder. "How did you get here?" Her companion looked in disbelief, but overjoyed, a spontaneous smile forming on his face. "Sendoa!" he said. "Thank the gods, you are safe!"

"I wanted to make sure you were fine, so here I am," he said in a stern voice, giving a nod to her companion.

The four guards were approaching fast, taking their swords out.

"We could do the next step of our wedding ceremony. That's another reason why I'm here, love." He tried to give her a genuine smile.

"Were you going to marry?" asked her incredulous companion.

She pulled a face of disgust. "We can't marry! What do you have to offer me? Sanescid? A poisoned wasteland? On the other hand, why should I marry the identical brother of a slave, looking the same? Disgusting!" The soldiers were almost there. "You might, though, replace him since he's gone," she smiled. "I do miss your brother, you know?"

Her companion didn't understand anything.

"I almost gave up my life thinking that you had died. Gods, I would have given it for a bitch!" he said, remembering how he had been willing to die for her. How dumb had he been! "If you'd been truthful, you'd have gotten so much more than you ever imagined. Now, you'll get nothing, not even my death."

Her companion then took out his sword, furious at the way Sendoa was talking to her, but did not move, still confused. Hadn't they been friends before? What had he done to her, he wondered?

As one of the approaching guards was swinging his sword at his head, Sendoa pushed the red button and disappeared. Beatrix screamed and ran away. Her companion ran behind her.

The guard that had intended to strike him paled. "It was a ghost!" It was one of the worst omens they could have seen. There was a ghost to revenge his death on them.

"I don't like this," said the second one. The others stood motionless. Their minds were racing, in total terror of the gods. They knew what their king had done to General Sendoa and knew it had been wrong. Now the gods were taking revenge, they thought. They looked from one side to the other. Nobody was around. They wanted to leave, maybe run away as far as they could.

* * *

Sendoa and David, looking through the projector, were wondering whether Beatrix had screamed out of fear or rage.

"I think rage," said Sendoa, saddened, but also curious now that he knew her real self. How could he have been so blind? Now, he realized how much she had hurt his brother, and how much she had lied to him since they were children! What part of her was real? Obviously, that which he had just seen.

Back then both brothers had felt each other's pains, but they hadn't known where they came from. Therefore, when Zigor had been in physical pain, Sendoa felt part of it. In the beginning he sent his thoughts right away, *What's happening nire lagun?* But he had discovered that it was not a good idea to communicate with him just then, for he usually felt more pain coming. So, he sent his thoughts of concern later. Then, Zig would tell him a little, but preferred to ask him things about his life, trying to forget his own misery. Sendoa then would tell him nice stories about others around him, because he, in other ways, was also miserable, missing his brother, and working hard to be a good son and soldier from a very young age. He had never been treated as a child, so he didn't know how to be one either. He used to tell Zigor about other children's lives. Sons or daughters of the people that worked in the palace. The ones he knew, or so it seemed to him, were happy.

Unlike him, they got toys for presents on their birthday. He was never given a toy. He received either weapons, which he'd have to learn to use right away, or books of strategy for war. Then he had to recite the books to his father. When he received a weapon, he had to show his father how it worked, sparring with much older men. The greatest present he ever received, although it was not meant to be, was his beloved horse. He also recited Zig his books on strategy and told him about his training, because he wanted Zig to be able to defend himself whenever he could. He tried to explain to him how to fight. He told him to visualize while he was training. He hoped then that maybe, just maybe, it would be handy one day, when either Zig could escape or when he could rescue him. Now he wondered how much Zig had really learned.

* * *

After the encounter she had observed between Sendoa and Beatrix, General Michaels was suspicious about the state of the town. She decided to discuss it with the King brothers.

"I agree with you," said John.

"The woman seems as if she were the host, when she should

be a guest of the people of this town," said David. "I wonder if the Heinneans invaded them."

"I want five scout ships to survey the town," said the general to Captain Flores. "Give me all the intel you can gather."

"Yes, General," said the Captain.

16

The Plan

General Michaels was right. Harten, the town, had been invaded by the Heinneans. The scout ships watched over the town in invisible mode and found that the natives had been enslaved, while the invaders had taken over their properties. *This is not acceptable*, thought the General.

"We need to do something, sir," she said.

"We sure will. You are in charge, General," said John.

* * *

They waited to attack at night, when most would be sleeping. Meanwhile, a few ships were flying silently, scanning the city and the fields. All the citizens of Harten seemed to be under the yoke of the invaders. The new immigrants had apparently been very aggressive, which made John more at ease with their intended actions.

After they gathered all the information they could, they waited.

"Still interested in going, Zig?" said Michaels, not convinced that it was a good idea, though she did agree that it was his right to decide.

"Yes, General," said Zig.

"Then, you have to promise to…"

"Be by Nick or Renith's side under all circumstances, Do not shoot in the head, to kill. Shoot only to the chest, so that they get sent to the mothership, unless under utter danger. If wounded, press emergency button. It's the one right here," said Zig, as if he'd learned it by heart, which he had. He showed his forearm, where there was a red mark on the military uniform he was wearing.

"Ok," she said, but she was still very worried.

"I promise, ma'am, I won't mess up."

"I know, Zig," she said, realizing that he was still feeling guilty about his PTSD episode earlier. "I just worry about you. We don't want you hurt! But I trust you."

"Thanks, and I know what to do if it happens," he said, touching his right thigh. If he pressed it, a dose of David's medicine would come out.

"Ready!" said the captain.

They were going in airships, similar to David King's "car", but equipped with guns. Each ship carried four guns: one attached to the front, one on each side of the ship, and one at the back. The gunners sat at the center. Renith was the pilot, Zig to his right, and Nick to his left. Either Nick or Zig would take the back gun if necessary. Since Zig didn't have any experience, he would let Nick take it. The plan was to get there without making any noise. There were ten ships flying in two lines to surround the city. The first line was going to scan the area, house by house, and listen to the inhabitants' thoughts. If possible, they would telecommunicate their intentions to the prisoners and the locals, hoping that they would trust them. The second line was the backup in case of surprises. Anyone resisting or attacking them would be shot in the chest, which would send them to the 'nether-room,' a huge space at the bottom of the mothership already prepared for the prisoners.

Bruno Marquiz, the captain, scanned the houses and larger buildings. Each house had around ten people, all chained to a bar attached to the walls. Each house seemed to have only one guard. All the guards were sleeping, confident that none of their enslaved prisoners could ever escape. Marquiz sent a message to the prisoners' minds: *We intend to free you, but you must promise to stay quiet and away from the palace. If you agree, send your thoughts thinking 'yes'.*

The shackled people that were awake were shocked at first, thinking that someone had talked to them so, they looked around. Not seeing anyone, some thought the words were spoken by their gods, whom they had been imploring for justice for a while. Had their gods finally heard them? They thought, *YES!*

Who can be your leader? Don't talk out loud, just think about him.

Most thought of the figure of a middle-aged man. He seemed to be a spiritual man named Francis Bertrand. He was well loved and respected by all. Most didn't know where to find him, but a few did. That would make it easier for the scouts.

Would you trust this man to decide for you, this time only? If so, think ... Before even finishing his thought, he was receiving everyone's answers, *yes.*

* * *

Francis Bertrand was tied, like the others, in one of the newer houses. He had been beaten and was breathing heavily. Bruno got into his mind and introduced himself. After that, he told Bertrand their strategy.

Francis woke with a horrible headache but understood what was happening. *How can I trust that you'll liberate us? You are probably the same scum,* he thought, but agreed it was better to give it a try. It couldn't be worse, could it?

We are Oksaleb, but not the scum that's helping the Heinneans. The ones that have helped these invaders are a small group of rebels. We are already taking care of them. I promise that we'll take the invaders away too, and we'll make sure they never come back. We worry about the slaves they brought. Are you willing to receive them as brothers?

I'd receive them with open arms, but many of them are so sick that most of our Hartean people might not agree. You'll understand that I would ask the community for decisions like that.

We are planning to take them to a place where they will have the opportunity to heal and thrive, but some might want to stay, maybe they are in love with a local, or for other reasons. How will you treat those?

Like brothers, thought back Bertrand. *We were people of love. I hope with all my heart that we continue to be so, if we are ever free again.*

You will, I promise. Meanwhile, try to rest. This morning you will be free.

Francis wanted to believe.

17

The Implementation

The ships had landed silently near the town. It was a quiet night. The sky was full of stars, not a cloud to be seen. Captain Marquiz finally gave the order: "Get in with maximum silence. Shoot the guards and free everyone that you trust. Leaders of each ship tell the prisoners that you are under the orders of their leader, Mister Francis Bertrand. Read their minds to make sure they are on our side. At the least doubt, shoot. We'll sort them later. Let's go!"

In groups of three to four, with their guns, they went from house to house. If the building was bigger, holding twenty or more prisoners the group would be of six to eight. The soldiers were disgusted at the amount of people shackled one beside the other without space for even relieving themselves. The air stank of urine and defecation. As they walked by the prisoners they learned that most had been the owners of their homes with their families when the Heinneans had arrived and taken over. The Hartenians were pacific people. They had solved their problems with their neighbors as friends, discussing any problems that arose. They had never imagined that this would happen to them. They believed in karma. This way of life had meant they were never attacked, on the contrary, neighboring towns usually came to them for advice. Now, their neighbors were terrified and had been looking for ways to defend themselves from the invasion. They hadn't dared to help the Hartenians, fearing that they were going to fall under these monsters' yoke too. They knew that the Heinneans were too powerful because they had the help of the Oksalebs. No matter how ashamed they felt, their instinct of survival was greater. The risk was way too big.

You sure we aren't killing these people as we shoot them? thought Nick. He was apprehensive, for he had committed to nonviolence since Rick's death.

Renith shook his head, then answered in sign language, *They'll end up in the mothership jails.* Then he moved his hand to the chest.

That made both Nick and Zig more willing to shoot without regrets, *to the chest.*

Renith had noticed that each smaller house had one guard, and that the bigger ones had two, amounting to one for around every ten shackled prisoners, he calculated.

With their night vision on, they could clearly see where the guards were and what they were doing. Most were drunk and sleeping. Some had an unwilling woman, boy, or girl with them, and only a very few were alert.

Their first house was among the small ones. They went to the guard and shot him before he even noticed anything. Then, Renith sent the captives the message, *We are here following Sir Francis' orders, to free you and get rid of these invaders. Please be as quiet as you can.*

The ones that woke up went dead quiet. As ordered, Renith

scanned their minds. They were a family of five, three neighbors whose house was probably being used for other purposes, and two foreign slaves, brought from Heinne.

Renith shot at the shackles on the prisoners' wrists. Zig and Nick then did the same as fast as they could. Once freed, the people were asked to wait until there was no Oksaleb rebels, nor Heinneans around. After that they would have their city back, the captain promised.

It went swiftly, and in less than thirty minutes they were surrounding the palace. Only then, did one of the guards notice something and sound the alarm, but it was too late. The Oksaleb were shooting every Heinnean soldier before they ever got near. The enemy archers had better luck, aiming flawlessly, but the arrows could not penetrate the Oksaleb soldiers' armour. Their night vision also helped them stay away from danger.

Zig aimed and shot, making each target disappear instantly. It was like magic. He had never used a weapon like this one. Actually, he had never used a weapon at all, so it felt strange. As he aimed and shot, he was getting better. As a matter of fact, his speed and precision were incredible for a rookie. He felt good shooting at the Heinneans, remembering how he and other children his age had been abused by them. He began to feel a blind rage, but then he remembered what had happened to him earlier, so he centered himself back, and continued to shoot as many as possible, trying to stop himself from feeling any passion. He wondered, though, about the ones who could be innocent but were being sent to the same place as the guilty.

"Don't worry. If they are innocent, we'll know," Renith shouted. "Better take all prisoners and sort them later, said the captain."

Again, someone reading my mind, thought Zigor.

Sorry, thought Renith back.

Zig actually understood. After his episode, he was okay with his friends reading his mind.

After around thirty long minutes, some soldiers put down their weapons and lifted their hands, "Please don't shoot," said one. Renith realized that the soldier thought all those who were shot were dead.

"If you are Hartenian and worried about your people in the city, they are fine. We freed them and you have no reason to fight us."

That made half of the soldiers turn around and either fight the Heinneans, or leave. It took no more than ten minutes after that to take over the castle.

"I don't see any rogue Oksaleb," said Renith.

"They are not here right now," said the Hartenian that had spoken earlier.

"Great!" said Renith. "It's better like this. What's your name? I'm Renith Solivan."

"I'm Rod, son of Munro."

"Nice to meet you, Rod." They shook hands.

"What now?" said Rod.

"This will be very easy for us. I think you should go to your family and community."

"Thank you, Sir Renith."

"Please, just Renith."

* * *

Zig was unwilling to go to the castle.

116

"There are enough of us getting into the castle. What would you like to do, Zig?" said Renith.

"Find the other slaves, the ones on Death Row, being punished. They should be underground," said Zig.

Renith communicated this to the captain. "The Captain asks if ten men are enough for that purpose."

"Yes. Thank you."

"I'm going with you, Zig," said Nick.

They searched for holes where there could be people, all around the castle. As they were walking to the back of the castle, for some reason, Zig knew that they were near one, and sure enough, the detector began to beep. The first thing they saw was a wooden trapdoor on the ground. One of the Oksaleb scanned the area and found traces of life. One of the men was about to open it when Zig stopped them.

"Careful, there could be a trap." He remembered how one had exploded once and killed everybody inside. Luckily (though he did not think that way at the time) he had been outside being physically abused by Beatrix, so he didn't die. Nobody knew what had triggered the explosion. Now he imagined it was probably a rat meddling with the trap.

The same Oksaleb scanned more meticulously, finding the booby trap. It was of their own making. *How disgusting it is to learn that our own people have empowered these monsters by bringing them technology that hadn't been invented here yet!* Zig thought. It was beyond belief. The same device deactivated the booby trap. Then the Oksaleb scanned again, at least three more times. Once completely sure, he opened the trapdoor and let Zig in.

"Thank you," said Zig.

The stench was so awful that Zig began to gag as soon as he

was inside, as did the others who were still outside.

"Zig," said Nick. "Get out and put on the mask first."

Zig put his mask on and turned his night vision on. It was awfully dark down there, darker than when he was with his brother in the clinic, but the goggles helped him to at least see silhouettes. The stench also stopped, except for what was left inside his mind. He went down a flight of dangerously rotten stairs that creaked alarmingly now and then. He was hoping to find people he remembered from when he'd been a child, though he knew it was practically impossible. The last time he'd been with them, he had been so young. However, he had a hunch that today he would find someone he knew and he always followed his intuition. As he saw signs of life, he used his gun to break the shackles and free the slaves tied to them, but kept going forward. The men behind him were helping by picking the prisoners up, and assessing how much help they needed. Nick was behind him, moving any dead ones aside. They would pick up the dead later, after they were sure that the living ones had a chance to survive. Most of the slaves were men of different ages.

"Is it you, my little Zigor?" said a woman's voice out of the gloom. Little Zigor. Only Lilith would call him so.

"Lilith? What are you doing here?" She was the sweetest person he'd ever met. Everybody loved her, even the slave owners. She had always protected him, even from himself. He went straight to where the voice had come from. There was a woman who looked to be at least in her late thirties, maybe early forties. It couldn't be her! When he was a child, she had seemed to be just a little older. Eleven? Twelve?

"You remembered us! I knew that you would come to save us! My beautiful little Zigor."

118

"Lilith, what are you doing here?" he said again.

She began to laugh. That laugh he remembered. "Oh gods!" It was so good to see that she was alive!

"You knew I was coming?" He had a smile on his face behind his mask. How did she even recognize him? He looked at Nick, who was not far from him helping a man and for the first time he realized that the masks were invisible.

He focused back on Lilith, zapped her shackles and hugged her. She was a bundle of bones, so he did it very carefully. Then he picked her up and got her out of that horrible place.

"Come on, I can do it by myself."

He let her go, but her knees began to bend. Zig held her, but decided to pick her up again, "Let me, please! How many times have you held me? It's my turn."

"Ok, my little brother," she said. "Only this time," and she hugged him.

"Hey, Zig? You can stay with her if you want. We can take care of the rest, don't worry." Nick knew that Zig wanted to make sure that every single one of these people was safe outside.

"Thanks, Nick!"

Outside the hole, Zig took the mask off. It was already dawn. He wondered how much time had passed. He saw David checking on each person and healing every ailment that he could. The sicker ones were taken to the mothership for better scanning and treatment. There were more Ewanians feeding them and cleaning them as best they could. Zig felt a rush of gratitude.

Lilith had her eyes shut. After being so long in the darkness, the outside was too bright for her.

"Why were you there, Lilith, and for how long?" That place

was for the most rebellious slaves. Most were left to die. They didn't receive food, nor water for days. If they survived, they were sent to work right after.

"I'm useless, my babies are born dead," said Lilith with a sad smile. "I'm cursed. What better than punish me for that and have me away from the other breeding women? My illness might be contagious."

He could read between the lines and saw the truth, the horrible, painful truth. She had killed every single baby she gave birth to and had made it look natural. She would never let them enslave any of her children, ever. He then realized that he had intruded into something personal, and blushed. When was he going to learn how to control himself? He carefully placed her on the floor and hugged her.

She pushed him off, "Dear, dear! You are going to get all dirty and foul-smelling! This is heaven! My boy, my sweet Oksaleb boy has saved me!" She was opening her eyes, trying to see him. "What a handsome young man you've turned into! Everybody was saying that you were dead, that the Oksaleb had cursed us, but I knew you were coming! They called me crazy, ha ha!"

"They sort of killed me, Lilith," said Zig. "The good Oksaleb managed to revive me, but I was as good as dead to the Thebans."

"Who are they?"

"The people at the last place I was on this infernal planet," he said, wondering if she understood the word planet.

But Lilith was exhausted and seemed not to be listening any more. "I think I'll take a nap," she murmured, and lost consciousness.

Zig looked around for help. David arrived beside him, "She'll be fine. Seems that she's emaciated, but not hurt."

Two Ewanians came with a stretcher.

"Where are they taking her?" Zig didn't want to let go.

"To the infirmary, like all the others in bad shape," said David. "Come with us, if you want."

Zig was worried about the rest of the slaves, the ones that hadn't been rescued yet.

"I promise we'll do a job as good as if you were here," said Nick. "I thought you trusted me by now." He was bringing out another skeletal, but still live slave.

He did. "Thank you, Nick. I owe you…"

"You owe me nothin', Zig. Being who you are and giving me the chance to be here helping is extraordinary enough for me."

Zig was very grateful, but didn't understand what Nick had meant. He let it go.

"What'll happen to all these people, Uncle?" They were rejected, outcasts. Most had suffered all their lives. What was there for them now?

"General Michaels sent some scouts to look for an idyllic place for them to start again. This planet has some virgin lands. Don't worry, they'll be safe," said David.

Zig was so thankful that he began to cry. He distanced himself from the others and covered his face, ashamed.

David went to him and hugged him. "Nephew, we're all very proud of you!" He also wanted to say, "You can hear the Oracle and follow it. You are our answer. Everybody is ready and willing to do anything you want, because you deserve it!" but restrained himself. He definitely didn't want to scare Zig away from his possible, and hopeful destiny.

Zig couldn't believe that they'd care so much for these people, his people, as much as this. He hugged his uncle back. "How can I thank you enough?"

"You have, son," said David.

At the infirmary, he saw Dr. Zelop connecting Lilith to a tube, so she could get some nutrition. She seemed unconscious still.

"After she's nourished, the tube will disappear. She won't even notice she had one."

Zig looked at the other patients around the room having different treatments and saw someone he had wished to never see again. The man of his nightmares. The one that had kidnapped him from Heinne and sold him when a child.

The man looked ancient, but he still recognized him. The mole under his right eye was the exact same. He was almost dead, with a ventilator keeping him alive. *What if I just pull the connection and let him go. What is this monster doing among the others, anyway? How did he pass the filter? Why is he almost dead? Is it really him, or did he just have a similar aura?* He decided to intrude into the man's mind.

He was indeed the kidnapper, but his mind told Zig an unexpected story. He visualized himself observed by the man. He felt the pang of pain in his chest thinking, *I can't let this child suffer with these rapists. I need to get him out of Heinne.* Then he visualized him grabbing the scrawny Zigor by force. Yes, he had to hit him so he stopped screaming or they would get caught. He put the child in a sack and took off fast.

Please, God of gods, take care of this child. If not for his sake, do it for ours, Zig heard himself say to a not convinced man outside the city, *Think of the curse! You owe me...*

Zig also learned that this man would have been willing to take care of him, but sadly Zigor was watched constantly. They would catch the man, punish him and punish the child worse.

The only choice he had had was what he had done.

When his own people came to get him, he was ready. At first, he had fought them, hoping to end up dead, but that hadn't worked. He got hit with a club and lost consciousness. The next time he woke up he had been beaten to a pulp. The following day they made a ceremony to humiliate him according to the rules. A noble like him was punished much worse than a regular traitor. He lost his citizen privileges. They took all his properties. Luckily, he didn't have family except for second cousins. They took his clothes off and made him walk through the main street across the city, where people threw rocks, rotten food, and even urine and excrement at him. After the horrible night Zig had been abducted, this man had been caught, enslaved and put among the lowest. Zig also learned that, ever since, this man had kept on trying to save others, putting himself in harm's way. He couldn't understand why he couldn't find the man's name inside his mind. *Maybe the ceremony did that? Maybe he thinks he's nobody, therefore doesn't deserve a name?* he pondered.

"Dr. Zelop," he asked, "does he have a chance?"

She looked at the patient. "Not sure, Zig. Is he important to you? Did you know him?" She would never get into his mind. He was learning every day that it was a matter of respect. He would try to learn the protocol and follow.

"Yes, he is, very," he said. *How can someone have no name?*

18

Bizitza Berria–New Life

Scouts had been searching for a place where all the rescued slaves could make a new life. They finally found one that, according to the Oracle, would not affect the planet's destiny. It was in another continent, far away from other people and it had everything humans could need. Captain Marquiz hoped it would be perfect for the beginning of a new life. The scout ships, now fixed for moving people, joined together to create something similar to an airborne train. The few healthier persons were the first ones to board, mostly men and women without children to get started with the preparations. The rear ships contained the food the Ewans had prepared for the first months, until they could raise their own. The next day they would be sending the rest, except for those who were still in the mothership infirmary. Everybody was very excited to see their new land, some smiling as tears fell, others breathing hard with wide eyes, others closing their eyes to breathe in the new air as they descended from the ships.

"And we will call it Bizitza Berria!" shouted someone from

the crowd.

Everyone yelled back, "Bay–yes!"

Zig was among that group, all teared up, passing his thoughts to his brother.

I want to be there, anaia*!* thought Sendoa back.

You will, brother. Tomorrow.

* * *

Both brothers were very busy helping people either finding natural homes in caves or looking for ways to build them. The first settlers had found a couple of caves where they would place the mothers and children, and the elderly. They were now wondering how they could help build more shelters.

"Do they know how to build?" wondered Sendoa. He, as a soldier, had knowledge of constructing temporary shelters. Zig had no idea, but he was willing to help in any way he could. He proposed a meeting among the settlers to brainstorm on how the city would develop and some very interesting ideas came out, as well as a leader.

Abarne Iturra, a perfect name for the father of all people. He was a natural, so respectful to everyone, to the point that Zig hadn't noticed how important he really was to everybody until he was almost beside him. Abarne was medium height, probably in his thirties. All these people looked much older than they really were because of all the suffering they had endured, so he didn't even try to guess. Abarne had scars that could tell a whole story. He had salt-and-pepper hair, and half his face had an old scar from a burn that had also cost him his left eye. People were surrounding him, either wanting to tell him their thoughts, or asking him questions. He used more signs than words. He probably had been their leader long before. What better way to communicate without their tormentors noticing?

"Do you understand what they are saying?" asked Sendoa of his brother.

"No." He had been out of Heinne so long ago. If he had stayed, maybe. On the other hand, he would probably have been dead. He had noticed that none of the kids abused like him were there.

Zig and Sendoa approached the leader to introduce themselves. People let them pass very respectfully, opening a space. The three were soon looking at each other.

Abarne noticed that the brothers were looking intently towards him so he walked to meet them. "My name is Abarne Iturra." He bent down in utmost respect, a bit unsure what these Oksalebs were expecting. He knew that this new life was going to cost them dearly. He just hoped that it was going to be better and not worse than before.

"Please, Sir Abarne, don't," said Zig, almost disgusted. "We're not worth this…"

"You absolutely are, master," said Abarne, "We now belong to you."

"You belong to no one!" gasped Zigor.

"You belong to yourselves," said Sendoa. "We are against slavery."

"We wish you to be the first people that will live in peace without enslavement," said Zigor. "I was a slave myself. I was sold or given away to Daedalus Heinne when I was a boy."

"The little Oksaleb boy!" said Abarne, "You were the one that gave…"

…terrible luck to a Heinnean who had tried to save me from those

126

monsters, yes I am, thought Zig.

"…the Heinneans crap! Ha ha…"

Zig smiled.

"Masters…"

"Please, don't ever call me that word. It's like an insult. Please don't!"

"Abarne," tried Sendoa, "we want to help. Zigor and I believe that you are a natural leader. We don't want to intervene in your new life, but we want to help."

"I'm not a leader," said Abarne and looked around questioningly. Everybody was looking at him attentively, ready for anything he told them to do. He blushed. "I'm not."

"Who would follow Abarne if he were your leader? Please raise your hands," said Sendoa. All hands went up. "I guess you are their leader, Sir Abarne. They respect you and would follow you anywhere."

"Anything you need and that is within our reach…" said Zig.

"Thank you," said Abarne. "We need to get the material to build. Who would like to go scout for building material?

About ten offered. "All right. Can you work together?"

They nodded. Zig and Sendoa went with them.

"We might as well scout and gather wood for the night." Another group of men and women formed.

After they had gathered wood and stones for building, a more knowledgeable group that had brought clay-like mud began to make bricks away from the rest; another worked the stones. All this kind of work had been done by slaves, which made them very good at building houses, roads, and anything practical to life.

By the evening the rest were already organizing the food from the ships. They had never seen food like that and were a little wary, though their hunger was stronger.

"This is a gift from us," said Zig. "It's ready to eat, so you can take care of other business, Mr. Iturra."

"Thank you," he said. "Let's give grace on a day like this." So they did. Then they gathered around a huge bonfire and shared the food. Zig and Sendoa didn't want to take their food, consequently they chose that moment to fly back to Harten.

* * *

"We are very grateful, Captain Marquiz," said Francis. "How is it that you came here to free us?" He did not believe in the goodwill of anybody, much less the Oksaleb. He still believed that his people were going to pay for the favor.

"Sir," said Marquiz. "Let me introduce you to General Sendoa and his brother, Zigor. Would you like to explain to Sir Francis how we came to help, General?

He caught Sendoa unprepared. "Sorry. Um, this is how it happened," and he told him about Beatrix's betrayal. "As you see, you are right. There was a selfish reason and we got what we wanted."

"So, you don't want anything from us?" said Francis.

"Actually, yes," said Zigor.

"And what is that?" *Here it comes.*

"You promised to respect the people who were brought unwillingly with the Heinneans that decide to stay. I ask you to keep that promise."

"I will. I don't know how many of them are staying, though."

"I wish there was a way of putting that on paper," said Zig.

"What's that?"

Marquiz stared at Zig, "They don't write!"

"We will do the ritual of compromise," said Sendoa. "Is that good enough, *anaia?*"

"That'll be fine," said Zig.

* * *

The next day Sendoa was too exhausted to even move. Only a few weeks ago he'd been practically dead, so it seemed that he had been pushing it too far. He had wanted badly to be by his brother. Also, for some reason he couldn't understand, he was having problems swallowing the food he ate. He knew that he wasn't getting sufficient nutrients. He promised to himself that he was going to talk with Dr. Zelop as soon as he could.

"Today you stay put, *anaia,*" said Zig.

"What are you talking about?"

"You look like crap. I don't think it's a good idea for you to come."

Luckily, John King was nearby to help. "Sendoa, you stay with me. I want to show you something."

"But—"

"There's a lot of people helping out there and I need you here today," said John.

"Trust me, brother," said Zig, "I know I'll never be as good as you, but..."

"You are fucking better than me!" said Sendoa. Then he realized, Zig had always been on the bad end: the unwanted, the trouble, the slave. He wanted to be better. How couldn't he see that he was on top? Everybody here loved him! "You know that Zig, don't you?"

"I'm not sure, *anaia,*" said Zig. "Let me show you that I also can ..."

129

"Sorry, I never meant..."

"I know, Sendoa. You are a great brother. You never mean me harm, but I need to prove myself. Love you, man. And eat, for the gods' sake!"

Sendoa, in reality, was grateful. There was not a part of his body that didn't hurt. It had been too much for him. "When do we start?"

"I'll give you a few hours of extra sleep," said John. "When you wake up, come to my office." He left.

Sendoa fought the need for sleep, but it beat him.

* * *

Four hours later, Sendoa woke up, actually feeling better. *I guess I needed that rest after all.* He'd been a general, in charge of all the Sanescid armed forces before the devastation. He'd been used to feeling responsible for every single man, woman, and child. Only the king had been his boss. *And a lousy one at that*, he thought. He'd left the responsibility of all Sanescid on Sendoa's shoulders, and he had miserably failed.

As he had promised his brother, he ate. He had to push the food in. *I'll talk to Dr. Zelop about this later,* he thought. All his bones still ached, but it was more manageable than earlier. He got up and showered.

"Good day, Grandson," said John as Sendoa was entering his office.

It felt strange: grandson. Was he really? John had the same mark as Zig's. David didn't have it, just like him. *I guess I belong to this family, after all,* he thought. He imagined that David's twin, Rick, had had it.

"Good day, sir." He wasn't sure what time it was.

130

"It's any time you want, we can move the ship at the time you wish."

"Sir," said Sendoa. "When is it acceptable to read someone else's thoughts, and when not?"

"Sorry," said John. "I didn't mean to. You usually read someone else's mind when you see them in deep trouble, you feel it. It's like they are asking you to. Also, when they are being questioned because they have lost all their privileges. Or, when you feel trust, like with a friend or family. I shouldn't have assumed that you trusted me, yet. Sorry."

"It's ok," he said. "I'm just not sure, I need to learn those etiquette rules, sir." He definitely did not feel himself as belonging to John's family yet, but he was beginning to trust them.

"Since you have been a general in Sanescid, I want to show you the ship and the weaponry. Come."

After looking at all the incredibly advanced technology, Sendoa felt like a nobody. He didn't know anything about anything. He didn't even know the word 'technology'! But he followed along. Curiosity was never absent in his nature. *Are you too busy,* anaia?

Never too busy for you, my brother, thought back Zig.

They are giving me a tour around the weaponry. Would you like to learn with me?

Always open to new learning, nire anaia. Zig was helping dig a ditch, a pretty boring task, which let him visualize what Sendoa was doing without difficulty. *Did you eat?* He'd observed that Sendoa hadn't eaten much while he'd been with him the day before. No wonder he was feeling so sick the day after. Seemed that Sendoa simply forgot.

I did, but please keep reminding me. When the tour is done, I plan to talk to Dr. Zelop about it.

Why? What's wrong?

I have a hard time swallowing.

Good idea, thought Zig.

General Michaels entered, "We ready for the tour, General?"

"Absolutely, General."

The weapons were beyond his imagination. They required a lot of mathematical equations to make a good shot, and he barely knew the basic operations, which was what every well-educated Sanescidian learned. The experience was making him feel stupid and, therefore, he was not enjoying it. *I definitely don't belong here. Maybe I could do better helping at Bizitza Berri.*

General Michaels noticed his discomfort. "Would you like to try this one? We can simulate."

He had no idea what simulate meant and was too discouraged. "No, thank you."

"Please, sit." She realized how he was feeling without having to read his mind.

He sat.

"You don't have to know all the math that regular people require for these weapons. You are a general, meaning, you are a very well-trained soldier. Give this a try." She was sure that he knew how to shoot arrows. She explained to him the basics: what button was for what and how to select different targets. "Try it. Don't pay attention to the numbers on your top right. You don't need them."

He aimed at the first target and shot right in the center, then moved on to the second and third. Perfect score. Damn right, he didn't need the numbers. He smiled. His intuition was good enough. Then the targets got harder, they moved, then faster, and zigzagged in more complex ways. He still kept his perfect score. He suddenly realized that he was having a great time.

"Now it's time to look at the strategic points to shoot at on enemy ships."

19

Salbat

ig looked as if he was daydreaming while still meticulously working on the ditch. He had done this type of work more than once as a slave, enough that he didn't have to think at all. In the past he had been connected to his brother, if possible, learning something new. This time it was just as easy. He was learning to use a weapon from Ewan, so exciting! His brother was the best! *How could you get that one?* he wondered. It was an impossible shot and Sendoa had hit it as if it was nothing.

Nire anaia, *let go and do it.*

Zig could visualize his brother's smile from ear to ear as the image faded. He smiled back. Then he saw the ditch that he was working on. *Not so bad, though I might have gotten a whip or more if they'd seen me stopping work and smiling, when, only two or three years ago?*

He looked around and realized that he was completely alone. 'Where is everybody?' Further away there was a group of men around his age looking at him and talking to each other. It reminded him of when he was a slave. In a similar situation, they might approach him and start insulting him. If they numbered more than five, they would beat him for the sake of it. It was supposed to be entertaining. If his master caught them, he would ask them to leave, and would beat him some more for being a sloth.

He carried on as if nothing was happening and continued to work on the ditch. As the group approached Zig began to tense, this time ready to defend himself. Now he was a much better fighter since he had had the chance to practice what his *lagun Ikusezina* had taught him.

"Are you the Oksaleb slave that made such a fuss that it got my little brother and other kids killed?"

Zig had no idea what they were talking about. He just looked at each of them, as prepared for the fight as he could be.

"Yeah," said another, "you are the asshole that provoked the deaths of all those children."

A third one then approached. He seemed skinnier than the other ones that had talked. "Because of you, all my family fell into disgrace," he said. "My sister was going to marry into a wealthy family, but she was taken away and raped by everybody. All because of you!"

Zig looked each one in the eye, tense, waiting for the attack. He was not going without a fight. Not this time, not ever again. He was ready. *Where are the Ewanians?* he wondered.

More people started to gather.

"What's going on?" said an older man who Zig hadn't seen before. He was helping an older, emaciated man walk. Zig recognized that one. The man without a name.

The younger men started speaking at the same time, and Zig learned that after he had been abducted as a child, in punishment, the Heinneans had killed all the children that had been sleeping with him.

Zig sat on the ground and began to cry. "Noooo!" He didn't care if they were going to beat him anymore. They had killed his friends, all of them!

"Stop!" said the emaciated man. "How dare you accuse him! I abducted him! He didn't choose to be abducted! Who knows how much suffering he has received from his other captors? How dare you treat this kid like that!"

The others scattered and left Zig with the man and his companion.

The man without a name got as near as he could to Zig, who was still crying. "You know it's not your fault. It's mine." He sat on the edge of the ditch, hanging his skinny legs down.

"Why did you do it?" said Zig.

"I couldn't stand what they were doing to you! A voice told me to, and I don't repent because I know it was the right thing to do."

Zig was inconsolable. He still couldn't see why he was more important than all those kids who were slaughtered. Why, according to so many, was he more worthy?

"Child," said the man without a name, "they weren't going to last more than a year, nor were you. At least I saved one. You."

"Thank you," he said, "though I don't think I'm worthy of so many dead children."

"All the bloodshed is not your fault, Zigor. It belongs to the Heinneans. Nobody else."

"What's your name, sir?"

"I have no name. I don't deserve to have one."

"If you don't want me to feel guilty for what happened then, sir, why don't you?" said Zig. "You saved my life."

The man smiled. "What name do you want to give me?"

"What about *Salbatzailea*—Saviour?"

"I think it's too much!" he laughed. "But if you want it, Salbatzailea it is. Let's make it Salbat."

Zig smiled at that, but then he got serious. "They hate me, don't they? They always will. I'm the cursed one."

"Nobody has the right to hate you, son. I won't let it happen."

"Sir, you can't stop them. It's okay. I hate this world too. I was just hoping that I could get a break here, in Bizitza Berri."

"And you will, I promise!" said Salbat. "Please, come with us, Zigor!"

"I can't, sir."

"Please!"

Zigor left the shovel and jumped out of the ditch. Then he held out a hand to help Salbat stand while the other man who had stayed quiet helped him, but fixed his eyes on Zig.

"So, you are the Oksaleb child!" he said softly. "Sorry about what just happened. I lost a beautiful little girl that day, but to be honest with you, I thank the gods for that! She died fast. Otherwise, she would have been raped over and over, then probably tortured by that little monster, Beatrix, her brothers or others, who knows for how long? She would have finally died after one, two, three years? I'm Luken." He stretched out his hand. Zig shook it.

"We need to report this," said Luken.

"Yes, we do," said Salbat.

"It's okay," said Zig.

"No, it's not," said Salbat.

"At least come, help me walk back to the eatery, so Luken doesn't have all the burden of carrying me. Please?"

"Yes, sir," agreed Zigor.

As they walked, Salbat asked Zig about his life, then Zig

137

asked Salbat about his.

"Eh," said Salbat, "not much of interest."

"I heard that you were a hero, sir."

"Where? How?" laughed Salbat.

"You'd put yourself in front of others to defend them, sir. Is it true?" Zig had read it from Salbatzailea's mind at the clinic. He hadn't talked to anybody except for Lilith and Abarne Iturra, their leader, till then.

"If they say so," laughed Salbatzailea. "It's all a matter of perception. You want to finish your misery, what better way than by putting yourself in front of everything that might kill you? As you see, it didn't work!"

Salbat did not let Zig leave the eatery. He made him sit beside him and talk about his life as it was now.

Luken excused himself. "I leave you in good hands, my friend," he said to Salbatzailea, looking at Zig. Then he made a slight bow and left.

Zig had no other option than to stay.

The eatery began to fill and get noisier. Everybody seemed so happy, chatting animatedly about their day. Many passed by Salbat to greet him and seemed very excited and appreciative about Zig's presence. They asked him questions and told him about themselves.

Somebody hit a gong, and everybody went silent.

"My dear friends," said Abarne Iturra. "It has come to my attention that something very disturbing has happened. I understand it involved a group of young men, and that they were Zadornin, Bardol, Peru, Palben, and Todor. Please stand up!"

They stood up, fixing their eyes on Iturra.

"You were threatening our friend here, Zigor, weren't you?"

138

"He killed my little brother!" said Palben.

"He ruined my life!" said Todor.

"I don't understand why you treat him like a highness, when he's the scum of the scum! An Oksaleb slave, what can be worse than that?" said Peru.

Salbatzailea stood up. "If you have any quarrel about what happened to you and your family in the past, it's with me! How dare you treat Zigor different to the rest of us because of a mark by his eye? Who the fuck do you think you are?"

Peru looked to the floor, but Todor looked Salbat in the eye. "You, Uncle," he said, disgusted, "destroyed my life. I hate you!"

"Stop," said Iturra. Then he looked at Todor. "If it weren't for your uncle, you would be dead, killed by the Oksaleb, thanks to all the damage your own people have done around this world. Zigor here hasn't done anything, except for saving our lives and bringing us prosperity. He is our friend."

Then he looked around and said, "Threats like those Zigor received will not go unnoticed. We cannot live with people bullying us. You four will be punished. I want to ask the rest of you how that should be carried out."

Zig wanted to disappear; he was so embarrassed about it all.

Salbat spoke then. "They should be shunned by the rest for a week and they should do special community service. It was so embarrassing seeing Zigor there, working on the ditch all alone while these punks were doing nothing but gossiping!"

"What do the rest think?" said Iturra.

"And ten lashes!" cried someone.

"No!" said Iturra. "We will not go back to whipping. No more corporal punishment, ever."

Most agreed.

"You four go have your food outside," said Iturra. "We don't want to see your faces."

"May I speak, sir?" said Bardol.

"Do."

"Zigor of Sanescid, I am very sorry for what I said and thought about you. The elders are right. From now on, I'll do my best to prove to you that I mean what I say."

The others looked at Bardol with hate.

Zig was looking to the floor, feeling awful. He really wasn't used to people apologizing. He wanted to belong. Sadly, he had no control over that. He looked in Bardol's eyes, "I accept your apology." Then he looked at Iturra, "May I leave, sir?"

"Please stay! Then we will know that you have really forgiven us." Salbat fixed him with pleading eyes, so Zig decided to stay. But he covered his face with his hands while the four young men left the eatery.

"Now, let's enjoy the great food our patrons have given us," said Iturra, looking at Zigor with a smile. Zig managed to smile back. He was stuck. Later, he realized that it was worth staying. Everybody else was so nice to him that he did feel a sense of belonging after all.

* * *

Bizitza Berri was looking more real with every hour that passed. They had traced where the different houses were going to be built, and some were already being constructed. The pregnant women, mothers with small children, and orphans by then had a place in one of the big caves. They and some of the other men and women were making the space as cozy as possible. The second cave was being occupied by the elders and the sick. Only the seriously ill were still at the mothership.

The Oksaleb had created a makeshift infirmary and patients were being taken care of by robo-nurses, making sure that they were stable. Lilith was still there but without a feeder. They wanted to keep her one more day as she was still very gaunt. She had made friends among the humans and robo-nurses.

Zig was flying on one last trip with Renith when he saw something, like a small sphere moving at top speed in the sky. "What's that?" he wondered, not being able to see clearly in the gathering darkness.

Renith looked in the direction Zig was pointing. "Fuck! That's not good."

Then they heard the first crashing sound erupt from the shadows towards what they imagined was their mothership.

"Hide!" called the captain. All the ships scattered and dug themselves underground as deep as they could, wherever they were, waiting for new orders.

20

Under Attack

"We have company," said John, "and they don't seem friendly. I recommend shielding."

"Prepare for defense," said the General through loudspeakers. "Shield, Cap'n."

"Aye, General."

Shielding the mothership was a way to prevent damage, but it also meant that they lost all communication with their people on Ethrea. Most of the crew was out helping the people of Harten and Bizitza Berri, because they hadn't been expecting any attacks. John was very confused, but the answers would have to wait. Now they had to figure how to defend themselves with only six crew in the huge ship. They decided to spread out at equal distances from each other and install the weapons they would use. The enemy ship was already shooting repeatedly, sometimes on different targets and sometimes the same. It seemed that their plan was to find the weak point.

Sendoa was still with Lina Michaels. "Please, let me use one of the weapons. I would not want to end up prisoner or dead without a fight."

142

"Here." She took him to one that looked very similar to the simulator he'd been practicing, so much so that he thought it was. "It's not a simulator, Sendoa." Again, she had not needed to read his mind. "We really need as many hands as we can. With you we are only seven against, who knows how many?"

"Sorry," he said. "It seems that I've been feeling too insecure and sorry for myself."

Michaels didn't have much sympathy in that moment. "It works practically the same as the simulator, except it's real. Put on this helmet so that we can communicate. Right now, don't shoot because we have the shield up. We need to find their weak point to shoot. Otherwise, we are doomed. You know strategy. The visor of your weapon will show you the characteristics of the enemy mothership. Look at it carefully and try to figure out its weak point. If you do find one, let us know right away. Any questions?"

"No, General," he said.

"If you have any, don't hesitate," she said. "I might take some time to answer because the others might be communicating too. Be patient. I believe in you, Sendoa." She nodded and left without waiting for an answer.

Sendoa began to check the enemy ship through the visor. He studied it bit by bit. Even though he barely knew anything about ships, he looked for something that would tell him something. Different. He wasn't sure what exactly. He finally saw something somewhat odd, that did not follow the pattern. Could it be a weak point after all?

"General, I think I know how to disable the enemy."

That was fast! she thought. In seconds she was right beside him. "Show me, General Sendoa." The shield of their ship was beginning to give and the vast craft started shaking from the

143

brutal bombardment.

He put a finger on the screen without touching it. "There," he said. "If all of us manage to shoot on that spot, more than one will get deep inside and destroy that?" It was a dark triangular figure braking the homogeneity, "Or am I wrong?"

He definitely wasn't, *It's the brain of the ship! She recognized.* She had no idea how he had gotten there without years of study. She had no time to ask questions either. It had to be done right then. "Good! I like it. Let's do it."

She communicated with the rest to explain the strategy and give the coordinates. "1100 south, 58 west, to the countdown of three. At two, open shield, shoot at one, after zero, close. Three, two, one, zero, close." The second the shield was open, a few shots got through, causing some damage. Luckily, they did not get to any vital part. However, the enemy ship broke into three piece and lost total control of its movement.

"Woohoo!" Sendoa heard through his helmet, scaring him at first as he wasn't sure what was happening. "Long live General Sendoa!" They were definitely beginning to believe in the Sanescid twins, or should it be the King twins?

"How did you do that? How did you get to that conclusion?" asked General Michaels.

"Just a hunch," said Sendoa. He had a huge smile on his face.

"Congratulations, General Sendoa!"

It was gratifying to be praised by important people from such an advanced culture.

21

Dr. Cray's Property?

"**B**ackup is coming, Dr. John King," said a voice out loud through the shielded ship. "That kid is Dr. Cray's property. It was an experiment and it's not human. It's a clone. Give it back and he'll press no charges against you or your crew."

Who is that talking and who is Dr. Cray? John wondered. It must be his son-in-law, the one that created the breach between him and his daughter. Are he and Marina there? He hadn't heard from her since the acrimonious farewell. As her father, he had her always in his mind, but it had to be her that was the one to reach out to him, since she had been the one to reject him and all her family.

He asked for a meeting in the lunch room with all the crew. "They still think it's only one of you," he said to Sendoa, "and I hope we keep them thinking so."

* * *

"What did he mean by clones belonging to Dr. Cray, sir?" asked

Michaels. "Is it *the* Dr. Cray?"

"I guess so," said John. "Seems that he manipulated Zig and Sendoa's genes, but they have my daughter's genes according to the files. I don't see any manipulation in the kids' genes."

Cray was considered a renowned scientist, who had been working on creating more efficient clones. He had had a lot of success in the use of them, but it had turned controversial since his subjects many times were a mix of humans and animals, sometimes different species of animals. There was a philosophical and ethical complication. Up to what point were these created beings considered human? How many human genes did they have to contain? John was repulsed that this man created clone mixes of human or animal genes at all, and could not understand how this was accepted without a doubt as if it were normal.

Zig and Sendoa, though, were clearly not clones.

When Sendoa was brought to the ship, Dr. Zelop had checked his DNA, which showed genes belonging directly to Marina and her husband, Dr. Gullivan Cray, in natural proportion. It was the norm to test them and be prepared in case of an emergency. Both twins were ordinary Ewanian humans.

General Michaels looked questioningly at John.

"Even if they evolved outside their mother's womb, they have natural genes from two humans, Gullivan and Marina. They are my grandchildren. Last time I knew, humans," said John. "On the contrary, what Cray and Marina have done is a crime punishable by the law. We cannot let these criminals take these boys."

Everybody aboard the ship agreed that they would not give up Sendoa and Zigor, they were willing to defend them if needed. Dr King was right. They were very human.

A new message came from the enemy ship. "The Oksaleb people don't follow you any more, John. Give the clone back and we will let you go without charges."

"What do we do, sir?" asked Michaels.

David, meanwhile, had been very quiet, thinking. "I want to help, brother. I'd like to talk to Amaranth and ask for help. After all, they are my nephews too." Amaranth was the governor of Elihc, the main state of Ewan.

"Please vote," said John to the assembled crew. All raised their hands in approval, though some were worried. What if they were the ones acting against the law?

"But this might turn into a civil war, sir," said someone.

"Let's hope not," said Michaels. Then, looking at Sendoa, "These kids deserve our care. Anyone against?" No hand went up. "Then let's open the west shield to communicate with Elihc."

David used his private phone directly to reach Amaranth Conde, the governor.

"David! What a surprise! What's up?" said Amaranth.

"I wish I could answer to that in a positive way, but instead, we are here orbiting Ethrea in a dilemma." David explained what was going on. "The Oksaleb seem to be siding with Cray because they don't have the whole story. We need backup or my nephew will be used as a lab creature. He's suffered enough." He sent her all the information they had gathered about Zig. They didn't dare talk about Sendoa, not even to her. He was still invisible to the Oksaleb; in a worst-case scenario he could get mixed with the people in Bizitza Berri and stay safe. Zig, on the other hand… They, or at least he would fight for the kid to his death, under the Ewan laws or not.

As David was explaining this to Amaranth, she opened the communication to all Elihcians as it seemed to be of great importance. First of all, nobody was allowed to mess with the destiny of any of the other worlds. This was a huge breach of the rules, punishable by a life sentence. It took a few minutes to get everybody interested in the case.

Elihc was the most important state of Ewan. It was the leader, which could compel all other states to comply if it demanded, therefore their say was heard. It was not an imposition, but it had great weight. Each state had its own government, but when differences were too hard to solve they asked for help from Elihc, and Elihcean propositions were almost always viewed as final.

Almost a hundred percent voted in favor of defending and protecting General Michaels" mothership, so it was decided to send the Mammoth. The Mammoth was a huge ship that could split into seven parts. It left at full speed.

Meanwhile, John was talking on his private phone to his second-in-command in Oksaleb at Epsion.

"Make this statement public, Carlos. You owe me at least this!" He was furious. How could his right-hand man go against him and not even tell him what had been happening? They had a direct line for these purposes! How had he ended up being accused of wrongdoing and discharged without being told? Maybe it was time to retire, but he hated the idea that that monster Cray and his own daughter (apparently, a monster too) would take over!

"Sorry, sir. When Dr. Cray explained to us what you'd done, we couldn't deny him his own right."

"The right to use and abuse a human being while accusing me of theft when I'm absent and cannot defend myself?"

"Said that way it sounds horrible! Somehow, he convinced not only me, but everybody. Now you have the right to express your point, sir."

Carlos called for an emergency audience. "Ready, sir."

"Dear citizens," John said, "I don't know how much you know about a private matter concerning a grandchild I have, who was abducted when a zygote, presumably by his own parents, and sent to Ethrea. Then, after being born, he was enslaved, abused, and would have been killed, if he were not saved by a ship I hired with my own capital." Since he didn't want to reveal Sendoa's existence he had just mixed both twins' stories.

"This is proof of what I say." He sent all the documents of Zig's life, with the videos they had from Mrs. Blight's dreams and some of Zig's. "On the other hand, your government, under Carlos Avenos, sent a ship, probably paid for by your tax money on a private matter and probably without your consent, because he believes that this infamous Dr. Cray has more say than you or I." He heard an uproar from the other end of the line. Good. "Now they're sending reinforcements, again with your tax money. Is that what you really want? I recommend you vote."

He waited. "As I said, this is a family matter and, therefore, I had not asked for your help. But I did ask for my brother David's after we got attacked by the ship you are paying for for this monster that calls himself Dr. Cray. David asked for help from the Elihceans who gave him their approval for sending the Mammoth ship. It's on its way to take Cray and his crew to the Elihcean court." He waited again. "This doesn't mean civil war. It's still a family matter. As far as I know, I'm still your governor, even if Carlos and the rest went against me behind my back. I need to know right now if I have your approval."

He waited for an answer. Momentarily, he thought that the connection had gone off, or had been turned off on purpose, but he waited.

"Dr. John King, we've voted on your behalf," said a representative. "We are furious that the government has been using our tax money for this. We do not approve of the ship going. We've shut off the flow of money and called the ship back. We are also charging Mr. Carlos and Dr. Cray for the money used on the first ship and we are already checking on your grandchild's information.

"Now we hope to have your approval: Mr. Carlos is stepping down, the people have voted for me to be the temporary governor until you are back."

"May I know your name, sir?" said John.

"Sorry! I am Raymond Black, sir. Do I have your approval?"

"You do Mr. Raymond Black, and I thank you."

"Thank you for letting us know what's going on, sir. When you're back, we need to look into a way of communicating better."

John knew Raymond well as a hardworking man and a good problem-solver. What worried him was that Carlos had also had those qualities. What was going on? How the Oksaleb had turned against him so easily was his real concern.

Sendoa had moved away, near to one of the 3D screens that were showing what was happening on the enemy ship. Everything seemed calm. The ship was broken into three parts, that were drifting apart very slowly, one of the side sections nearing the planet. It seemed that the enemy had no control over the ship.

What does it all mean? he wondered. Were they clones, for real? What was a clone? Did that mean that they didn't have rights as human beings? Since the interested party didn't know of his existence, he was safe, but his brother… He couldn't let anything happen to him, he had to do something.

"Don't do anything stupid, Sendoa," said David.

"Why the fuck do you feel you have the right to read my mind any time you want?" He was furious.

"When I feel danger coming, I don't respect the protocol." said David dryly. "If you shoot and kill Cray, it will go against you really ugly. Then nobody will be able to save you or Zigor. All our efforts will be for nothing."

"So, if he wins and they define us as 'clones', which I have no idea what that means, but it seems like it could be slavery or worse, being the property of someone…"

"I won't let that happen, Sendoa," said David. "I promise, but if you kill the monster, they might accuse and charge you with murder. Then you will go to jail and be far from your brother. All of us here want to protect both of you. Please let us do it."

"Look," said Sendoa. There were small ships flying out of the enemy mothership, straight to Ethrea.

22

Meanwhile in Ethrea ...

"**A**ttention, enemy ships are incoming. Shoot to destroy if you need to," said the captain.

Around twenty ships were approaching at full speed, shooting at they went. In Bizitza Berri trees were being destroyed with the firing and the people were distressed and terrified. The enemy were approaching the caves. The ships that had been hiding began to shoot back. Renith and Nick were very busy returning fire already. They had thought that there was no time to train Zig, but they didn't know that he had been learning how to shoot through telepathic link to his brother's training, which made him more at ease. He checked the weapon at his disposal and discovered that it was quite similar to the one Sendoa had been using. It had the mathematical system, but he could also use it with his own senses. He looked at the speed and direction the ships were taking and anticipated their route, then shot a few blasts. He destroyed one after another incredibly fast. The other ships changed direction, away from them, but towards the new town. Zig, as if in trance, reprogrammed his course, shot another few blasts and destroyed three more. The rest decided to fly away. Five others were falling from the shots of the other ships. Three turned around and headed directly at Renith's ship like kamikaze. Zig, again as if in a trance, shot back with a speed nobody had imagined directly at a missile aimed at them, while Renith tackled the ship that had shot it, and Nick fired at the ship behind them. The shots completely disabled the enemy, and the ships fell to the ground. The very few left untouched returned to their mothership. However, the fallen ships could still shoot, so there was a tense silence for a while.

The captain finally said over the loudspeaker, "It's over. The Mammoth ship is here to pick up the rogue Oksalebs. Surrender or we'll shoot to kill." The Oksalebs left their broken ships with their hands up.

23

Humans or Clones?

We were never humans, after all. Or were we?
*That's what they say. We're clones created by
someone called Gullivan Cray.*
I can't go back to slavery, brother!
We won't. What shall we do? We need a plan.
*Before we lose our freedom. Actually, right now, I'll begin a
hunger strike.*
We'll begin a hunger strike. Let's meet at your room.

When the ships came back, they were received with cheers.
The Mammoth had already arrived and were taking the
renegades on board. John had decided to go with them to
explain the situation and make sure that Cray did not twist
everything again.

When Renith, Nick, and Zig left their ship everyone cheered
even louder, if that were possible. They'd been watching
the battle and were mesmerized. They didn't know who the
amazing shooter had been, but soon they would. Renith and
Nick lifted their hands in triumph. Zig was pensive. Right
after they passed the crowd, Zig excused himself, went straight

154

to his room and locked it. Sendoa was already there.

After reviewing the battle, everybody was astounded. Some had thought the incredible shooter had been Nick, after all, he was the only person they didn't know. To their relief, it hadn't been him. It had been Zig! They all looked at Renith, surprised.

"You taught him, Ren?" said David.

"No, sir. I had no way of training him with weapons."

"So, Zig. Zig? Sendoa?" Only then did they realize that the brothers were not there.

* * *

David knocked on Zig's door. He'd tried Sendoa's already. "Zig, Sendoa, you guys there?" His phone rang. It was Zig.

"Sendoa and I are not getting out of this room until we get our freedom. We don't care if we are fucking clones or not. No matter what your court decides, we are humans before the Oracle. We don't belong to anyone. If we are not respected as such, we are starting a hunger strike, and if anyone tries to come in, we'll shoot ourselves in our heads. Understood, Dr. King?"

"Zig," said David, "we are on your side. We voted to protect both of you no matter what."

Silence.

"Why don't you trust us?" said David.

"We do, but if the court decides that we are property of that Dr. Cray, you will follow suit."

"We won't," said David. "You are my nephews. I won't let anything happen to you. Don't you see?"

Zig did see and believed him. Sadly, it was one against

a whole world. "I do, sir, but you can't fight alone." He disconnected the phone.

"Sendoa, you can save yourself," said Zig.

"No, brother. We won't get separated again. Whatever destiny we have, we'll face it together."

Zig took out his art tools and began to draw out how he was feeling. Sendoa lay down and fell asleep.

By nightfall, Zig noticed that Sendoa was very pale and his breathing was shallow.

"Sendoa... You okay?"

"I don't know. I don't feel well."

Zig noticed for the first time that his brother was actually all bones. "You're still emaciated! Why haven't you eaten?"

"I have! It's just so hard though. It gets stuck here"—he touched his chest—"then it comes out. I can't control it."

Zig called Dr. Zelop. "Sendoa's not well and he's freaking me out. Could you please come, but alone?"

Dr.Zelop walked through the small crowd standing in front of the brothers' room. She felt the tension. She knocked on the door and Zig opened it, quickly closing it behind her. "You know that they can make that door disappear and get in?" she pointed out.

Zig had no idea and did not care, so worried was he about his brother. "What's happening to him, Dr. Zelop?" Sendoa by this time seemed semiconscious. "It looks like he's starving!"

She checked the vitals and scanned Sendoa. "I think I know what's wrong, but we need to go to the clinic," she said.

"Okay," he said. "Please wait." He grabbed his gun and placed it on the bed by Sendoa's feet. "Let's go."

The doctor fixed the bed in floating mode so that it could be used as a stretcher, opened the door, and pulled the bed through while Zig pushed. On the other side were half of the crew, those on their break. They reverentially made space for them to pass.

Seems that David's words were true, thought Zig, No one followed behind them. "Thank you," he said out loud.

Sendoa's stomach bottom sphincter had closed, not letting the food pass through. Apparently, the healing treatment had not progressed as expected, and, since they had been so busy, nobody had remembered to check on how he was convalescing. For his part, Sendoa thought that what was happening was normal. Eventually he would be able to hold the food. Then he got used to just throwing up, thinking that some of the food must be coming in at least. He had planned to ask the doctor later, always later.

The doctor put something similar to a stent into Sendoa to open the pylorus, the muscular valve at the base of his stomach. He was so emaciated that he had to be fed through a tube, at least for that night.

"Zig," said Dr. Zelop, "we are with you. Let us be with you, please!" She gave him a dish containing chicken and salad. "Let us love you. Eat."

"Thank you, Dr. Zelop." He ate. The chicken salad was delicious, or maybe he had just been starving. Maybe it was too soon and they should start their hunger strike later. 'It feels so good to be cared for by so many people!' He never imagined this—it was confusing, but it felt good at the same time. As long as he was free to end his life on time, it would be fine, he thought.

24

The Trial

"**Where are the prisoners? Has anybody delivered justice?**" asked Sendoa. **He was** wide awake, tired of lying in bed, feeling much better than he had for a long time.

Zig looked at him, not understanding at first. What was he talking about? "Oh, yeah!" The prisoners that they had captured in Harten. "I hope they are rotting down in the basement, except for the innocent ones. I'll ask David." He was wondering whether the pilots were together with the Ethrians. Later he learned that the Ewans were on another floor.

All the Ethrian prisoners had walked through a behavior and lie detector. The ones that had no bad history had been freed to wherever they wanted to be, with the commitment of being good citizens and never letting their community accept slavery. Most had been soldiers who had had to follow orders or had families themselves and had worked for the Heinneans to protect them from slavery. A few had been servants and decent people in the wrong place. About a third were in the guilty category.

"We need your help with those ones," said David to both

brothers.

"How can we help?" said Sendoa.

"Don't count on me, *anaia*," said Zig. "They can all go to hell as far as I'm concerned." He knew that the Ewanians would never do that, and that was the reason he wasn't interested in helping.

"It's okay, Zig. You can go your way," said David. "Let's go to the viewing room to watch the interrogations," he said to Sendoa.

Sendoa looked at Zig.

"I'll be in the room working on my new drawings," he said, and left.

* * *

"That one is one of the men that captured me and sent me to Tebas," said Sendoa, remembering how he'd trusted in Beatrix and followed her advice. Now he knew, it had led to his doom. Funny that both brothers would have died in the same city if it hadn't been for the Ewans. Born together, separated all their lives, then together in their brush with death. Happily, they were together now. Damn, he needed Zig to declare who had tortured him! *Won't happen*, he thought.

They had seen about fifteen people whom Sendoa had not met before. Most of them had been following orders, though they had enjoyed it. They were granted their freedom after promising to go back to where they had come from, do community service, and to never enslave anyone. They were shot with a chip so that they could be watched for a few years. If they broke the oath they would be exiled a faraway island. For now, unless the inhabitants of Harten agreed that they could stay, they were to return to their own country.

Then there were the perverts and sadists.

"So, death sentence?"

"I'd like to ask him some questions, sir."

"Go ahead."

Sendoa reached the microphone. He didn't want the man to see him. "What's your name and rank?"

The man was scared to death. A voice coming from some place, from the ceiling was talking to him! Was it a god? He had so much to pay for! "Grut Bau... G-general of Platoon Number 9," he said.

"Grut, you've tortured innocent people, you've raped girls as young as eleven years old, you've killed people for sport," said Sendoa. "Do you have anything to say in your defense?"

"That's how things are supposed to be at my status! I-I couldn't behave different!"

"Who created those laws?"

"King Daedalus of Harten, sir!" said Bau.

"What happened if you didn't follow the laws?" said Sendoa.

"My status would be reduced to the lowest level," said Bau.

"And now I am to decide your fate, whether to put you to death or give you some other punishment for the rest of your life, Bau," said Sendoa. "Some who I'm following advice from would wish you an agonizing death. I think you should suffer all the suffering you inflicted on others, one by one. Then I'd throw you somewhere in isolation, far away from anybody you ever met. What do you think, Grut?"

Bau was bent in a corner crying for mercy. "Sorry, I didn't know, please...!"

"What can we do to this type of monster, Dr. King?" said Sendoa, away from the microphone.

"I like your idea of having him pay exactly what he did to others and sending him to an isolated place. This planet has islands where we could leave him to stay forever alone," said David. "Let's do that."

Sendoa felt disgusted. "Who's going to torture him, and rape him?"

"Oh no, son. Nobody will do that to him! Sorry, I didn't explain myself well," said David. "He will do it on his own. It's like living it through dreams. He'll never, ever want to do something like that again."

"But then, if he's never going commit those crimes again, shouldn't he have a chance to go back to his community? He'd be harmless, wouldn't he?" said Sendoa.

"That would be your decision to take, but I wouldn't tell that to him until you're sure he deserves it."

"Okay, sir, let's do that."

That was what they did with most of the prisoners left, since their deeds were similar. Both Sendoa and David were exhausted by the end of the day.

Zig had been making drawing after drawing all day. He had them scattered all over the place; the bed, desk, chairs, floor. He was working on another when there was a knock on the door. He knew it was Sendoa. "Come in," he said, trying to move some of the drawings from the floor by the door.

Sendoa looked at the pictures spread everywhere. He picked one, then another, and another. They were the features of the people he and David had been judging. Somehow, each picture showed the soul of the accused. Sendoa wondered if Zig had been there with them, helping in his own way. "Brother," he said, "I really need you with me there!"

"I've been with you, Sendoa," said Zig. "Please, don't let them

161

see me! I'd be pleased to help you from here."

It was true. The pictures Zig had drawn revealed the most hidden secrets of each accused. With them, he could know better which punishment each deserved. It was even more precise than what Sendoa had been doing with David.

"You have only two to do tomorrow: Beatrix and 'Uncle' Daedalus."

"Oh crap!" said Sendoa. "I can't deal with them! Please help me, brother." Then he remembered that Zig had PTSD. "Forget what I said. If you can, draw pictures like you did today. They will be very helpful."

"Let's sleep on it tonight?"

"Okay."

There was a knock on the door.

"Come in," said Zig. What the hell? Was all the ship going to visit?

"Please open the door! Hands full." Nick was carrying a huge tray with lots of food. "You won't deceive me. I know neither of you have had anything to eat for a while."

"Yeah we have! At the clinic." But they were perfectly happy to eat more, especially Sendoa, whose stomach had literally opened.

25

Interrogation

"**W**hat's your name?" said a voice from the wall. "Who the hell do you think you are?" said Beatrix. "I demand to talk to Dr. Cray!"

"What should we do with this one, Sendoa?" said David leaving the loudspeakers deliberately. He wanted her to hear the conversation.

"Sendoa!" she said. "It was a misunderstanding, please help me and I'll marry you! You'll have all the lands we've conquered and the Oksaleb on your side!"

"Why the fuck did you do that, sir!"

"Oh, sorry, kiddo. I didn't know that you didn't want her to know that her life depended on your whim of the day," said David. He was good at sarcasm, no doubt, to the point that Sendoa couldn't keep his anger.

"Sendoa, Dr. Cray will find these renegades and punish them! Set me free and you won't have to worry about repercussions!" She was feeling stronger, more confident.

"Could you explain to the bitch the whereabouts of her Dr. Cray, sir?" said Sendoa.

"With pleasure." Then David told her how her protector was being judged, and that he and his people were the renegades. All were going to pay a high price for intervening in Ethrea's destiny, which had been a completely unacceptable act.

"Let's start over, shall we? Your whole name, please."

"Beatrix Heinne." She said it very quietly.

"Beatrix Heinne, you are accused of torturing children from a young age. Then sending others to torture and kill innocent people of all ages because they wouldn't or couldn't comply with your every whim. You are an accomplice of the enslavement, torture, and death of the inhabitants of all the villages your father has invaded, by giving him ideas on how to be even crueler," said David. "What do you say in your defense?"

"That is gossip from people who don't like me!" she said. "Ask Sendoa how good I was with his brother till he was kidnapped!"

"When your father decided to rape him, oops, sorry. Your family called it *initiate* him. You gave him a beating for being as dirty as the others, Miss Heinne. How is that good?"

"How do you know that!" she yelled. "You can't read my thoughts! That's not true!"

He knew it was true because of Zig's thoughts, but he couldn't tell her that. Since she thought he was dead, it was better to keep it that way.

"You know it's true. Cut the crap, miss," said David.

This was the weirdest thing David had encountered. Beatrix Heinne was the only person he could not read. It was as if she was from somewhere else, but her genes clearly came from Daedalus and Laura, her deceased mother. She must be one of Cray's experiments, thought David. He sent all her dossier and the interview as it was happening to Elihc's governor. "What punishment should we deliver, Sendoa?" said David.

She began to yell and curse, promising all kinds of hell against Sendoa and the rest of the ship's crew.

"I agree, sir, that she should live every one of her deeds in herself."

"NOOO! You have no right!" screamed Beatrix.

"So be it," said David, 'Then we don't need to know what she did or did not do. It'll come from her own mind. Then what?'

"I don't think she should have a second chance, sir."

"I agree, Sen," said David. "We are preparing a safe place to deliver the worst monsters. They shouldn't ever be free again."

"You loved me, Sendoa! How can you treat me like this?"

How could he had ever loved her was the better question. He felt nauseous.

"You sent him to his death, Miss Beatrix! How can you expect anything better from him?" said David.

"But he's not Dead!" she yelled. "You are not dead!"

Sendoa began to gag, so he left the room in a hurry. How on earth had he ever loved such an abomination?

David followed behind. "I'll take care of her father. Same punishment?"

"Same, unless you think he deserves different…" he said. "Excuse me." He ran to the nearest bathroom, still gagging.

Not a good idea, bro. You had surgery only yesterday. Let's go to Dr. Zelop. Zig was out of their room and running after him.

* * *

"All seems to be working well." said the doctor, "but you should take it easy, Sendoa. No more stressful work for today." Then she looked at Zigor. "You, take care of your brother. Don't let him get near the prisoners. I understand that there's only one more person waiting for judgment."

"Daedalus Heinne," said Zigor.

"No, Dr. King is dealing with him already," said Sendoa.

"Good," said Dr. Zelop, "and if there's any others you need to impart justice to, you take care of them tomorrow, only after you've come to me."

"Yes, ma'am," said Sendoa. He was emotionally exhausted and didn't want to deal with anyone else. He was so much better a soldier than a judge. He still felt upset that Zig had not helped him, but then he remembered why.

"Let's have lunch, now," said Zig.

Sendoa's stomach reacted to the word right away. It seemed that his appetite was finally catching up with him.

26

"We Want The Truth, Cray!"

"Hello?"

"Hi, Amak.*"*

"Zigor! So nice to hear your voice! How are you?"

"I'm well. You? And Mr. Blight?"

"Trying to redo my life. It's so weird to be retired! So, what's up?"

"Is there a chance that me and my brother could stay with you, Amak?*"*

"You are always welcome here, my son. I hope you are not in trouble."

"I'm not sure yet."

"We'll see how we can help. I don't think that anybody, no matter where he comes from, could just make you disappear. You are a famous artist in this world."

He wished...

When the Mammoth ship arrived there were many people waiting for Cray. About half of them were carrying signs saying "Cray, we are on your side" or "We can't believe what we are seeing. Please explain!" The other half was furious. "Cray, the poster boy. Show your real self!" "Where's your wife?" "What did you do to your child?" Or simply "How could you!"

Cray had been a very popular researcher. Everybody had respected him as one of the most efficient applied scientist and technologists of the moment. He had been working to create efficient machinery by using cloning, with clones created practically handmade to any specific need. The product was so far from humans or known animals that they were considered machinery, depending on the use they were supposed to have. He had only had a few detractors, mostly fanatics that proclaimed that even a gene, no matter how manipulated, deserved to be respected as life from God, or The One.

Now his popularity was crumbling. Everybody had had the chance to meet Zigor through the images that David had sent. Such a charming young man, so human, so similar to Cray too! Even if he was a clone, which everybody doubted, since he didn't show the marks, he was too human! Cray had no right to claim this youth as property! They read the genetic outcome, which revealed that he was Marina and Cray's natural son. Cray's most devoted followers were crestfallen. How could someone use his own child for experimentation? They needed an explanation. That's why they had come out with their signs, trying to make sense of all this.

"Dear friends," said Cray, "You know how much Marina and I have given to this world and look how they are treating us!"

They could see him on a screen that manifested in the air. His grey eyes were mesmerizing. He could turn around a crowd just with the intensity of a look.

"Cut out the bull, Cray," shouted one of his people, "we want the truth!" Many agreed.

"All will be cleared up in court," said Cray. He seemed very cocky, and he was right to be. He'd done what nobody had ever dared to do. He was so respected that nobody had ever questioned him before. This was going to turn horribly against the Kings. That made him feel even more arrogant. It was a wish he had had for so many years. Maybe this time they would finally be finished!. He waved at his followers and got into the ship that would take him to the court. It was already late so they would start the questioning the next morning.

27

Cray's Trial (Ewan)

Sendoa was suddenly awake, He looked at the time: 5:10. Then he saw what had awoken him. "Zig, it's too early! What are you doing?" He promised himself that it was going to be his last time sleeping in the same room with Zig.

"Sorry, brother, I had a dream. I must put it on paper before the trial begins."

"About what?" asked Sendoa.

"The Oracle," said Zig. "When I'm done, I'll understand better what it means. Right now, I'm at a total loss."

* * *

"Please state your full name, sir," said Judge Hammond. The court in Ewan was very different to those on Earth. There was a judge and two officers to help. Anyone who wanted to see what was going on could watch proceedings through a screen that appeared just in front of them, and anyone that wanted to question the accuser, as long as he or she had been involved in the case, had the right to do so. There was no need to figure out if someone was guilty or innocent because the lie detectors did the job. They had never failed, to the point that nobody now ever questioned their use.

"Dr. Gullivan Cray, you are accused of tampering with a foreign planet, of kidnapping your own son when a zygote, then, of abuse and neglect by not doing anything when the child was given as property and by letting his slavers mistreat and rape him, despite knowing where he was. Not only did the King brothers bring the evidence but the lie detector confirms it."

Everybody was watching the trial.

"I don't understand the accusation, Your Honor," said Cray. His tone was warm and soft, his eyes intense on the judge, his hands tied behind his back. "I've given my life to science, to making our lives better. This male looks human, but it's not. I will shortly explain why, and also will explain the type of experiment he was created for, but for the moment, I need to have him back."

The judge didn't like what was happening. He felt that Cray was right, but it didn't make sense. He turned to look away from Cray and focus on the topic.

"Please, Dr. David King, present the evidence that Mr. Zigor is not a clone."

David, from the mothership, introduced Zigor through the screens. "This is Zigor." Zig made a small nod. "We'll do the test right now, to show everyone." He took a metallic object, soft to the touch, and passed it over Zig's face, then his arms, hands, body, and feet. All the time it read Zig's genes and interpreted them as an average of 50% belonging to Cray and 50% belonging to Marina.

Cray turned white. Then he looked to the floor. "I don't understand! My son died in the womb." Then he mumbled something that nobody could hear.

"There are no marks of manipulated DNA. This is a human being, Dr. Cray."

Cray looked straight into the judge's eyes. "I'm innocent. You must let me go."

The judge seemed to be struggling over whether to let him go. It was absurd! He remembered that Cray had been brought in for something, related to what they had been talking about, but he couldn't remember. What was it?

"May I talk, sir?" It was Zigor. His voice was soft and calm. It made the judge wake up from the trance he hadn't realized he was in.

"Yes, please!" said the judge, relieved, looking at him through the screen.

"I had a dream last night—"

"What does that have to do with this?" said Cray, furious.

"You had the chance to talk, Dr. Cray," said the judge, his eyes still fixed on Zigor. "Please continue, Mr... Zigor."

"It, the dream I mean, came from the Oracle."

The Oracle. Very Ethrean. "You mean God?" he was about to say, but then remembered that Zig had lived in Ethrea all his life. How would he refer to divinity, otherwise?

"It said that Mr. Cray..."

"DOCTOR Cray!" yelled Cray. Everybody watching was broken from the trances they had been in and saw a very angry and ugly face for the first time.

"SHUT UP, Dr. Cray," said the judge.

"...is able to control people through his voice and eyes. He is able to hypnotize when he talks, and enchant us with his

172

powerful gaze," continued Zig.

"What?" said Cray and started laughing. "It's ludicrous!"

"Have you ever checked his work as you usually would do with any scientist of his category?" said Zigor, to everyone. His voice was soft and welcoming. Everyone was listening. Cray's trance was over.

"What should we do?" said the judge, more to himself. Then he called one of the guards and told him something nobody heard. "Dr. Cray," he continued. "Please close your eyes."

"NO!" Cray retorted. "I have my rights!"

"It's not a request, Dr. Cray. It's a command."

Cray not only did not follow the order, but instead looked intensely at the judge and said in his soft, dreamy voice, "No."

The judge avoided Cray's eyes. "Do it now, Dean." Dean, the guard, was behind Cray, holding a black fabric bag. He put it over Cray's head and tied it at his neck.

"What are you doing? This is unacceptable!" Cray was trying to get his hands loose so as to take off the bag. "You brat!" he yelled towards the screen, towards Zigor.

"Me, a brat?" said Zigor in his soft, calm voice. "I was born in the wrong place, marked, beaten up since I have memory, given away as a slave when I was probably three years old, raped, kidnapped, sold again. Used as a mule to carry heavy loads. Finally, starved and beaten almost to death. On the other hand, you, Dr. Cray, have been able to do absolutely everything you have wanted. Who's the brat?" As Zig was describing his life, his mind recreated some of it and it was projected for everybody to see. It was something that he had not wanted to do, but he knew that he had to use every means to beat such a powerful man. With great embarrassment, he let it happen. Everybody was shocked.

"Okay," said the judge, "It is clear that Dr. Cray will have to pay for his crimes. Any other questions or comments? I wish the public that's seen the whole trial to discuss the punishment, if we are done."

"I still have a question for Dr. Cray, sir. May I?" said Zigor.

"Do so."

Cray was fuming, unwilling to respond to any question Zigor asked.

"Where is my biological mother?"

"Hah," said Cray, "she, obviously, doesn't want to see you! She's not here because she hates you all." He tried to use his soft and calm voice, but it cracked a little.

"The Oracle in the dream told me that she was confined in Dr. Cray's laboratory at Oksaleb."

"What?" said the judge, and many people watching gasped. "Send people to check what's going on in Cray's laboratories." Then to Zigor, "What is she doing there? Is she alive?"

"It told me that the place has to be checked as soon as possible. It wants Dr. John King in the team. I couldn't tell you how she is. The only one that can do that is Dr. Cray, sir."

"Dr. Cray, answer the question, please."

"She's fine! She doesn't want to see any of her family"—the lie detector began to flash— "especially her father! I'll not allow intruders in my labs!"

"You have no choice, Dr. Cray," said the judge. "We'll have a lunch break for now and we'll wait for the findings in the labs. Dr. Cray, you and we know that you are lying." He excused himself and left. The screens went off.

28

Cray's Cloning Labs

The team was already at the doors of the labs with the warrant. If the employees had planned to try and hide anything, they had very little time. At the entrance, someone approached the team and shook hands with John.

"Good afternoon, Doctor. I'm Terry Gibbens. I wish to help you move around Dr. Cray's building. Where do you want me to take you first?

Sergeant Saramiego was not happy that this Terry Gibbens talked to Dr. King, and not to her. Then she understood. Terry knew why Dr. King was there. His daughter.

"Take me to my daughter, please." He glanced at Saramiego.

"I recommend we split up, but I don't want you to be alone, Doctor," she said.

"You are the boss, Sergeant. I'll follow your advice."

She split her team into three groups. Then she went with King.

They went to the lower floors, which immediately aroused his suspicions. What would Marina be doing there unless she was working? That was his hope.

Gibbens led them to a corridor to the left, then to the right, then straight. It felt like a labyrinth. King was wondering if they would ever get out without Gibbens' help. *How many people could die trying to get out of here?* All the doors were closed and looked identical. They couldn't see through them. They didn't have names, nor numbers. Gibbens finally opened one of them with a key, walked into another hall, to the right, then to the right again, and to the left. On each side, as before, there were doors, but this time you could see through. They all looked like labs, with tissues or organs of different sizes inside aquarium-like boxes. All the rooms were very dark. Gibbens walked them to the end of the corridor and unlocked yet one more door. This room was dark. It had a human-sized aquarium, and a silhouette could be seen floating.

King looked at the figure, then to Gibbens, "Where's my daughter?" He didn't want to accept that that was his daughter.

But Gibbens pointed to the aquarium. "There."

"Pass me a pair of night goggles." He didn't want to believe it.

Gibbens passed him a pair. It was the body of someone that could be his daughter, alright. He focused on her face. Her eyes were open, but she didn't seem to be there.

"Is she in a coma?" said King.

"Yes, sir," said Gibbens.

"Since when?"

"I don't really know, sir," said Gibbens. "She's been like this since I came to work here."

King was shocked. "How long have you been working with Dr. Cray?" he said.

"This is my fifth year, sir," he said.

"Judge Doss, do you follow?" There was no answer.

"Why isn't there any reception, Mr. Gibbens?" said King.

"There's never been reception here, sir." That was very convenient for Cray.

King couldn't feel his daughter in this person inside the aquarium, even though she looked very much like her. Maybe because, after all the years passed, he was imagining her looking older, more like a 40-year-old woman, and this person looked to be in her twenties. He couldn't feel her essence either. He always had, for the gods' sake she was his daughter, after all! Now he felt nothing.

Suddenly, he felt something, but not from the woman in the liquid. He felt the need to get out of there and follow. Follow what? Something. Something was pushing him to go out of there, so he did. It pushed him to walk back from where they had come, to the right, left, straight, but then to the right and down the stairs. It was all even darker there, but as he stepped on the floor the lights turned on. There was a long corridor with only one door at its end. Gibbens and Saramiego went behind him.

John stopped in front of the only door and waited. Gibbens passed him, put his hand in front of the handle, and the door unlocked and opened as the lights turned on. John could see that it was something like a morgue. His daughter was dead. He felt the energy pushing him again. By then, he knew it was his daughter's spirit that urged him on. His eyes began to hurt and he noticed that his sight was bleary. Only then did he realize he was crying. Some tears spilled over on to his cheeks. He kept on walking until he was in front of a cabinet. The door had a lock protected by a code. John entered a code he knew to be correct. It opened. She was there, frozen. Parts of her body were missing. "What the hell?"

He had been recording all the events through his eyes and phone since he had realized that there was no communication with the outside world.

Talk to me, baby!

* * *

On the upper floors they could get reception again. "Sir," said Saramiego, taking him out of his thoughts. "We need to talk." Then she guided him away from the rest.

"It seems that Dr. Cray has turned the trial around. I've been asked to take you into custody as the prime suspect for your daughter's murder. I don't know how he did it."

"He's genetically modified himself to manipulate us all. My family has been more times than less in jail for being accused by manipulators like this one, but Cray seems to be the worst," said John. "Here," he added. "I recorded this trip. If you care for me..." As he heard the words come out he realized they sounded too selfish, so he tried again. "If you care for my grandchild, Zigor, which I dearly hope you do, take this." He passed her his phone. "I recorded everything since I realized that I couldn't connect with Judge Doss. I want you to keep it and use it when you really think it'll make a difference."

She did care for John. She thought that he was the kindest person in the world, and that he was a very good governor. She would do it for both of them. *Where can I hide this, though?*she wondered. They would, obviously, check everything she had.

"If you obey the orders without questioning, they won't," he said. "Sorry. I have no right to get into your head. I'm too nervous, sorry."

"It's okay, sir," she said. "I don't mind." She put the phone in one of her inner pockets. Then, she took him to the police headquarters.

29

Obey, In Spite Of?

I want to remind you that, if you get caught, we go together.

If I get caught, you'll flee as fast as you can, so you might have a chance of freeing me, brother.

That was not the deal.

The deal was that we commit suicide, but if I get caught and I lose that chance of killing myself, you must be non-existent. The fact that nobody outside knows you are alive is our only hope, anaia.

"General Lina Michaels," said the voice. "I recommend that you obey my orders here from Elihc. Otherwise, you are in contempt of the law."

Michaels felt compelled to follow without a doubt. Except for a slight headache that was beginning from the back of her head, she found the orders absolutely normal. She'd just learned that Dr. Cray was the new governor of Elihc.

"Yes, sir," she said, and closed communication.

The minute the communication ended, she wondered, *What the heck was that? Why would I obey this person who's not even Elihcean! What is going on?* She called for a meeting with her subordinates and Dr. David King. For most Ewanians, David had been their natural leader.

"I just got a call directly from Dr. Cray ordering me to come back and turn in Mr. Zigor Sanescid," she said. "As I was listening to it, all seemed normal. But as I turned the connection off to prepare the flight back, nothing made sense any more."

"This means that he took over by force, using his power of persuasion," said King.

"What do we do, sir?"

All eyes were on him. "I'd rather we ask Zigor," he finally said. "He's the one that has connection with the One."

"So, what do you think, Zig?" asked Michaels.

"I've been dreaming a lot lately. The Oracle tells me things I didn't understand until now," he said. "It told me about the Mammoth ship coming to us and gave me the instructions of how to disable it."

He looked at General Michaels. "It told me to ask you to go as fast as we can to Ewan and extract Dr. Cray from the governance building. It even explained to me in detail how stuff works, stuff I've never seen except in my mind. It told me that if we do this, Ewan may be saved. I have no idea from what!" He breathed in and let the air go out. "It finally told me to tell you, Dr. King, that you are right. A good pair of earplugs will help the headaches go away. Then they could ask techs to fix the earplugs so they don't have to hear the vibrations that Dr. Cray emits through his voice, but they can still communicate with each other. Again, I have no idea what it's talking about, except that, yes, Dr. Cray uses something to lure everybody to do his bidding, apparently through his voice."

David had actually already been theorizing on how to beat Cray's power of persuasion and had been observing Michaels' erratic moves and her strange headaches. Zig had the gift. Poor kid. It was a gift nobody, or at least he would not have appreciated.

Everyone looked at Zig in wonder.

Suddenly, David's phone rang, "Hello? Hey, Merrit, how are you!! …Yeah? So, almost everybody is having horrible headaches? …Yeah, same here. Try earplugs… Yeah, on yourself first. Check how it goes and try them on your patients. You don't believe me? Ha ha, let's bet!" He looked at Zigor and smiled, "Let me know how it works. Ha ha, good luck with that, good friend! Bye." Then he looked at the General, "First acts of resistance from Elihc."

Dr. Merrit had been a friend of David since they were kids. He was so focussed on his patients and his work that he never paid attention to what was going on around him, except in that moment. Somehow, he had felt that his friend David was in danger and that it had something to do with the headache epidemic.

General Michaels now understood what had happened to her. Dr. Cray's voice had lured her to do what morally was wrong and made her think it correct. Her brain did not agree, then it had reacted with a headache. The harder he'd pushed her, the stronger her pain. The only way to prevent that happening was to cut all contact, so she turned to the communications officer. "Lewy, turn off all communication to Ewan and the other ships."

"Yes, General."

"What's next, boss?" she said with a smile, turning to Zig. "How do we attack the Mammoth if we need to? Show me how we're going to disable it."

Zig spread out a long sheet of paper on which he had drawn the Mammoth ship during the night. He apologized that his tool was so primitive. These people had probably never seen or used paper. It could be compared to drawings in the caves millions of years ago!

"Don't say that, Zig," she said. "This is so cool!"

"Here's the back and left side of the ship, and this is the front and right side."

While she was looking at the blueprint, she took out the controls from her pocket and turned them on. Then she scanned for the Mammoth ship three-dimensional blueprint to compare it with what Zig had drawn. It was the exact design, very impressive.

Zig looked at the design that was now displayed in the air. Then he indicated three particular parts. "We must reach these three points to shut it down, but at the same time, prevent killing anybody. These are the coordinates that we must aim for. If we divide the shooters into three groups, each aiming at one of the targets, it should work."

Everybody nodded. It made sense. "At what distance should we shoot?" asked someone.

"Ideally very near. This would be the program," and he inserted all the information he had dreamed. It didn't really make sense to him, but he saw how everyone nodded and agreed that it was a very good idea. "The plan is to get as near as possible, then turn on the shield. They then will shoot at us with everything they have, but our shield will stand. There will be a pause of a few seconds and they will feel very confident. That's when we open the shield and shoot only once, all at the same time, on our already programmed targets."

It seemed so simple that a few were worried. The general didn't find any flaws, but it was good to have a backup plan if things didn't work out. "If it doesn't work, we'll shield waiting for their next barrage and fly full speed straight to Ewan. Knowing a little about the Mammoth, we'll do some damage, trust me. I like it. Okay, time to decide who's going to shoot what." She chose the best gunners, three for each group.

"Zig and Sendoa," she said, "you two seem to work well together. You'll be in charge of the left side with Nick."

The brothers were thrilled to be in the group, but then Zig wondered if it was just because he proposed the plan.

"You were fantastic down in Ethrea! That's why."

Michaels studied Zig's input on the blueprint again and decided the exact locations to aim at on the Mammoth ship.

King's phone rang. "General Munoz, what a surprise! ...Okay, you should be speaking with General Michaels. Here she is."

"Hello," said Michaels. "No, General Munoz, we are not giving up Zigor. Yes, we disconnected all communication because I won't obey orders from a usurper. ...When did that happen? They voted for him? How? ...Do you have a headache, by any chance? ...I figured." She passed the phone to Dr. King.

"Hello... You are a good man, General. We thank you... We'll think about it. Yeah, I've received calls... Put on earplugs, you'll feel some relief. Give it a try. Bye, sir."

King looked at General Michaels.

"We go to Ewan, now. If we surprise them, we'll have a better chance. Full speed," said Michaels.

They reached light speed in seconds and were soon standing, cloaked, not far from the Mammoth ship.

"Let's get to the precision points, in three... two... one...

now!" It was very tempting to give the command to shoot, but it was too risky. She preferred to follow Zigor's Oracle. "Shields on!"

The Mammoth opened fire, as expected. It was very scary to be there, trusting the shield would stand when so near, but it was working. The moment they had the pause the shooters were ready.

"Three... two... one... shield off, OPEN FIRE!"

They did in unison, and put up their shield again, as planned.

The Mammoth ship seemed to tremble, and then cracked into three parts, seeming to start to move adrift of each other. The broken sections continued shooting, but as they did, each part began to slide away and have difficulty aiming. Finally, they stopped shooting.

"I see scout ships coming out, General!"

"Let's go to Ewan at full speed. Do not respond." They unshielded and left at full speed.

David's phone rang. He turned it on for all to hear. "Hello, General Munoz."

"Give me General Michaels!"

"I'm here, General," she said.

"You traitor! How could you do this to your own people!"

"Do you mean fight for freedom from the tyrant you are obeying without question because it gives you a huge headache if you do, General Munoz? Or do you mean by defending the rights of a young man who's been abused all his life?"

"Put on earplugs, General Munoz, and tell your crew to do the same," said King. We'll send help as soon as we can." He hung up.

The ship prepared to move to light speed and left.

"Now what?" said Michaels to Zig.

185

"The Oracle said to trust you, General."

"Ok, we'll head at full speed to the government building at Elihc, then. Let's see how much our presence there will be a surprise.."

It was going to take them a day and a half even going at light speed. The central operatives would know by then that the Mammoth was disabled. They were probably going to be received on red-alert mode, which Michaels found very scary. She had never had the experience of fighting an actual war. This looked very much like it would be the real thing. She had learned different strategies at school and had been a good strategist in simulation exercises, but this was different. On the bright side, it would be the first time for everybody.

* * *

As the ship reached Ewan, they sent a message on repeat. "Please stay out of the way. We do not want to hurt anybody. Put on earplugs for your headaches. Thank you." That type of prerecorded message was all that could get through once the ship was shielded. They had maneuvered it so that it would stand exactly on top of the government building, at the thermosphere, about a thousand kilometers away. Small ships surrounded them and began shooting. It seemed that they would never stop. The plan had been to wait for a break, as they had when attacking the Mammoth. Then, instead of shooting at the building or the attacking ships, they were going to throw a bubble shield programmed to fall onto the building and surround it, isolating the target, Dr. Cray. No death involved. But it now seemed that the attack they were receiving would never end. The small ships took turns again and again. Since they were not going anywhere, they were willing to wait forever if necessary. After many hours, there was a tiny let-up and they tried executing their plan. The bubble fell and they managed to shield the ship again. Then it was a matter of waiting some more. Sooner than expected, though, the attacking ships left and a signal came from the last ship. "It's over. Dr. Cray is dead. You are free to come or go."

"What the heck happened?" said David.

Epilogue

The basement was piled with Zig's art. Aileen and Ulrich were wrapping each piece and putting them in boxes, as carefully as possible, following the instructions they had received for such delicate work.

"It was fun to have them here a while, but I feel better now that Zig's taking his work with him," she said.

"Yeah. If we'd messed up only one, we wouldn't be able to pay for it…"

The doorbell rang. Ulrich went to answer it and found two identical Zigors, one with a big smile, the other very serious. There were two reasons Ulrich could tell Zig apart: the mark by his eye and the huge smile.

They hugged as if they'd known each other forever, like family. Zig had never felt so good. He introduced his brother. "This is Sendoa."

Ulrich stretched his hand out to shake.

Sendoa gave a small nod but did not offer his hand. Ulrich put his in his pocket, feeling odd. *These kids!*

"Please, Sendoa, be nice. Thanks to them, you are alive!"

"Sorry Sir," said Sendoa, and stretched out his hand. "I'm learning this culture. I hope not to hurt your feelings."

It was true, but it was also true that Ulrich symbolized the figure of Father. He reminded him of King Kuiril of Sanescid, in stature and demeanor.

"It's okay," Ulrich shook his hand. "Feel yourself at home." He led them in.

By then Aileen was behind him, already pushing past to hug Zig. "Sorry, we haven't finished wrapping your pictures!"

"It's ok, ma'am. We should do it," said Zig. Even though he was so happy to see them, he was becoming shy, again. Who was he to call them his parents, after all?

Aileen noticed that he wasn't calling her *amak* anymore, but it was okay. He shouldn't ever have to if he didn't feel like it. She also noticed coldness in Sendoa. She guessed that having such a bad experience with their own parents was the real problem. It was good enough that both boys were safe and together. She had been circumstantial. They had probably come only to pick up the pictures. Nothing else.

"Do you want something to drink?" she said.

"Yes, please!" said both together, then Zig laughed.

"Something to eat?" she said. "We have chicken and salad."

They looked at each other and both said, "Yes, thank you!"

Okay. Food might be the ice-breaker, thought Aileen…

* * *

"We learned that one of the scout ship pilots that had been shooting at us couldn't stand her headache any longer," said Zig. "All of them were having excruciating headaches as they were shooting. She decided to fly down to the government building and fired three shots through the window where Cray was standing, while screaming, 'I CAN'T STAND YOU ANYMORE YOU MOTHERFUCKER! IF I END UP IN HELL, AT LEAST IT WON'T BE WITH THIS FUCKING HEADACHE!"

"And the 'motherfucker' died," said Sendoa, with a shy smile.

"We had the shield up all the time, so other than receiving a lot of strikes that felt like tremors and fearing that the shield eventually would break, we had no idea what was happening outside."

Zig stopped and looked at Sendoa.

"Suddenly all the ships that had been giving us their best shots, left. The last one left us a message in space, 'It's over, Dr. Cray is dead.'"

"I know I shouldn't feel this, but I was so glad!" said Zig. "We were planning to capture him through what they call a 'bubble' and keep him there where he couldn't ever hurt anybody again..."

"But with someone like Gullivan Cray, who had manipulated everybody all his life and got away with murder so many times, we couldn't believe that anything would ever stop him," said Sendoa.

"I personally thank the woman that shot him. She'll be in my heart forever."

"So, what's next for you two?" said Ulrich.

"We plan to stick together for a while."

"In Ewan?" asked Aileen, a little sad, imagining that this day was going to be the last time they'd see them.

"No, *amak*," said Zig, "we plan to stay here for a while."

That gave her an involuntary smile.

"After I won a prize in Munich, I've received invitations to exhibit in New York, Spain, France, Seattle and..."

I couldn't believe Victoria, she thought. *This city is too small.*

"...Vancouver, British Columbia."

Made in the USA
Monee, IL
28 August 2020